FORGIVING SKY

Forgiving Sky

Copyright Jenny Glazebrook, 2016

Published by Jenny Glazebrook

www.jennyglazebrook.com

Gundagai, NSW

Typesetting by Book Whispers (www.bookwhispers.com.au)
Cover design created by Kremena Petrova (k_petrova84, elance).

National Library of Australia Cataloguing-in-Publication entry (pbk)

Author: Glazebrook, Jenny, author.

Title: Forgiving Sky / Jenny Glazebrook.

ISBN: 9780992536398 (paperback)

Series: Glazebrook, Jenny. Aussie sky ; 6.

Dewey Number: A823.4

FORGIVING SKY

Aussie Sky Series

Jenny Glazebrook

To my daughter Merridy

My merry melody, my happy song
Thank you for your input and ideas for this final book
You make it richer and deeper just like you do our lives.

With thanks to Pastor Chris McRae who God used many years ago to deepen my understanding of forgiveness, and to Anne Hamilton whose book, God's Panoply *opened up a whole new world and understanding of the concept.*

Chapter One

Pounding feet were coming in her direction. Starre lifted her head at the familiar sound. Bruce raced past, flung open the truck door and threw his boots and bag into the back.

He paused a moment to call out to her. 'We have a call out to a property just north of Riley's Gate. Horse caught in barbed wire.'

Horse? Her heart began to pound. She tried to push the feeling back down, but Bruce had stopped and was looking at her. 'We need you.'

She hesitated, but only for a moment. A horse was in need. She couldn't refuse to help just because she'd be stuck in a truck with Bruce and …

Jordan shoved past her and threw himself into the rescue truck.

'Hey, Jordo.' Bruce poked him. 'Move over. Starre's coming too.'

Jordan's eyes lit up and Starre looked away. On second thoughts, the horse could survive without her. 'Sorry Bruce, but I haven't finished feeding the dogs.'

Bruce's thick grey brows drew together. 'It's an emergency. They can wait.'

She avoided his eyes. 'I don't think they can.'

The truck door squeaked open further and she knew Jordan was hopping back out. 'Look, if this is about the other day—'

She shook her head. It wasn't about the other day. It was

about the week, the year. And so much more.

Bruce was glaring at Jordan. 'What'd you do to her?'

'Nothing.' Jordan's expression turned sheepish. 'Well, I might have tried to crack on to her a bit.'

Starre snorted. 'A bit? You think?'

Bruce was studying her intently. 'Starre, whatever is going on between you two, can we forget it for now? You're the best we've got and this horse needs help.'

Starre focussed on the sign down the side of the truck. Animal Rescue. Was she going to rescue or not? She looked from Bruce to Jordan in indecision, then moved quickly toward Bruce. 'I'll come if I can drive and you sit in the middle.'

Bruce's brows rose, but he gave a quick nod and slid into the middle of the bench seat. 'Let's go.'

Doors slammed and she moved the truck into gear. She focussed her thoughts on the horse. It would need to be settled first. Barbed wire could cause serious injuries. She'd put a horse down before because of leg injuries and she'd never recovered. She wanted to close her eyes but needed to focus on the road.

Please God, help me save this horse. She missed Steadfast Ever so much it hurt. Her circus horse could have been saved if only she'd had the training she had now; if only she had understood more about lameness and found help earlier. She sighed. Her life was so full of if onlys.

She was vaguely aware of Bruce and Jordan talking. They may have been speaking to her, but she was focussed. Focussed on the moment, and the horse in need, and on keeping past memories from her mind. The latter was the hardest but she had done it for many years now. It had to get easier, didn't it?

She eased the truck into third gear and it bounced along the rough dirt road.

She barely registered Jordan's quiet words to Bruce. 'Ask her why she's still single.'

Bruce chuckled. 'Mind your own business.'

'So you know?'

'Maybe.'

'Come on, Bruce. I need to know what I'm up against here.'

Starre grimaced. Did they think she was deaf? 'I'm not interested in a relationship, Jordan. Believe me, you don't want to go there with me.'

Her words silenced them both. It seemed her message had finally got through. She threw them a dazzling smile. 'Directions, please?'

Bruce sat up straighter and cleared his throat. 'Um, yes. Left when we get to the huge Moreton Bay Fig tree.'

'Anyone there waiting for us?'

'No. The owner is in rehab. Had a major accident, according to his partner. Hasn't been able to tend to his horse. The partner was keeping an eye on Regal Zion for him.'

Starre stiffened and her heart came close to stopping. 'Regal Zion?' Her voice squeaked.

She was aware of Bruce's gaze on her. 'Yes. The horse's name, apparently.'

Suddenly she couldn't breathe. *God?* Had he done it for her? Ten years she had been looking for Regal Zion. She had never forgiven her brother for recklessly selling his beloved circus horse to some stranger. The first few years she had still held out hope. The next few years she had begun to doubt. And for the last few she hadn't even let herself hope anymore. At first working in animal rescue seemed the easiest way to locate Regal Zion. She had thought it would be a temporary job, but it had grown on her.

And maybe it had all been worth it. Her heart beat a crazy rhythm in her chest.

'Hey, whoa. Slow down.'

She glanced at Bruce. 'Sorry.' She hadn't realised how much she'd sped up. The truck didn't like the dips in the rough road.

Every second brought her closer. She hardly dared believe it could be him. Through her mind flashed the picture of her brother, Prince, standing on Regal Zion as they cantered around the circus ring to the sound of admiring applause. It seemed like such a long time ago. And then there was Chase. She drew in a sudden breath as pain cut her heart. She couldn't let her defences down like that.

'There.' Bruce's voice sounded in her ear and she squinted, following the direction he was pointing. Too far away to see yet.

She pulled to a stop at a gate and Jordan jumped out to open it. She eased the truck through, wishing she could drive off without him. But whatever she felt about him, she had to admit they needed him. He jumped back in and only just managed to slam the door shut before Starre had moved off again.

She was aware both men were looking at her, but she could only think of Regal Zion. She had to get to him.

'Behind the shed.'

She moved the truck forward as close as she could get. All that was visible was a horse's leg. But it was clearly caught in barbed wire. And it was brown with a white sock. Like Regal Zion. She slammed on the brakes, flung off her seatbelt and threw open the door. Every muscle urged her forward until she stood before the horse. His head was slumped, his legs hopelessly caught.

She let out a cry. 'Oh, Regal.'

He turned and big brown eyes looked at her. It was him. So much older and in bad condition, but it was his markings, his eyes. The magnificent creature was suffering terribly. He tried to move to her, but she was there first, flinging her arms around his neck, tears streaming down her face.

'Regal Zion. It's okay. I'm here.'

She was vaguely aware of Bruce and Jordan staring at her, but she didn't have time for explanations.

'I'll stay here. You two start snipping the wire.'

Bruce didn't question her. Regal Zion moved his head from side to side as though he couldn't get close enough to her. He threw his head over one of her shoulders, then the other. All the while she whispered his name and softly spoke to him, stroking his nose once so velvety and now so coarse.

Bruce's voice came from near his back legs. 'Keep him as still as you can. This one's the worst.'

Starre nodded, refusing to look and letting the tears continue to flow unchecked down her cheeks. She couldn't bear that Regal Zion was in such pain. He flinched but she continued speaking softly, reassuring him.

Finally Bruce stepped back, flinging the roll of barbed wire away. 'Done. Jordan, put the wire in the shed.' He moved to Starre's side. 'He needs antibiotics and a tetanus injection immediately. You up to it?' His eyes told her he wanted to ask questions; to find out the story, but he would give her time to tell it.

Tetanus. Starre took a deep breath. Peter Pan had died of tetanus and the loss of the horse had broken her. If anyone was going to give Regal Zion the lifesaving injection that Peter Pan should have had all those years ago, it was her. 'Pass it to me?'

Bruce nodded and pulled out her medical case. He drew up two syringes and gave them to her.

'This is because I can't lose you now I've found you again,' she whispered to the horse. He didn't even flinch as she administered the injections, then rubbed his neck. He seemed content to stand perfectly still, soaking up her familiar presence.

'I need to clean the wounds and stitch and bandage them, but I think we need to get him back to the shelter to do it. I can't restrain him properly here.'

For the first time Starre looked closely at the horse's back legs. They were a mess. If they put him in the truck like this he could damage them more. 'We can do it here. I'll keep him calm.'

Bruce's brows rose. 'He knows you that well?'

She smiled. 'Yes.'

Bruce didn't question her. He simply nodded. 'We'll do it now, then.'

She nodded, watching as Bruce sent Jordan to the truck to get more supplies.

Bruce set up, then looked up at her. 'About to give the local.'

She nodded. 'Go ahead.'

Regal Zion didn't seem to notice. His gaze was on her, and hers on him. Love welled up inside Starre in a way she had thought it never would again. Something in her heart had healed.

Jordan stood back, watching Bruce clean and stitch the horse and throwing curious glances at her in between. Starre tried to keep the amused smile from her face, knowing he was bursting to ask questions.

'He was my brother's circus horse.' She said the words gently, as though crooning to Regal Zion, but knowing Bruce and Jordan would hear. 'He was named after his father, Hope of Zion.'

The horse let out a snicker and she rubbed her hand tenderly up and down his blaze.

'My brother's name is Prince, that's why they called the horse *Regal* Zion. Prince …' she gritted her teeth. *He's an idiot, but I won't say that.* 'He sold Regal Zion.' *Among other things. Like getting a circus girl pregnant and then abandoning the baby. But that was years ago. He's different now.*

'So this horse was a performer?' Jordan sounded doubtful and though she resented it, Starre could see why he was dubious.

'Yes. He's a magnificent creature. He just needs a bit of tender care. And I'll give it to him.' She hesitated. 'Do you know what happened to his … his new owner?'

Bruce glanced up before wrapping the final bandage around the horse's leg. 'Nah. Some kind of accident that's left him in rehab.'

Jordan looked up from the bandage he was unwrapping. 'Maybe fell off a horse?'

'Well, it wouldn't have been Regal Zion.'

Jordan let out a laugh. 'So you say, with all confidence.'

She glared at him. 'Toddlers have fallen beneath this horse and not been trampled. He senses every move his riders make.'

Jordan's mouth tilted on one side. 'Ah, but every horse can be given a fright.'

Starre straightened her back and spoke stiffly. 'Regal Zion has stood still amidst gunshots, whip crackings, unpredictable crowds, applause, all manner of sudden noises.'

Jordan leaned back and let out a full belly laugh. 'Listen to her, Bruce. She's gone all formal and professional on us.'

Starre bit back a sheepish smile. It was true. She had taken on her debating voice and spoken properly to put Jordan in his place. She hadn't debated since high school, but the skill had returned quickly when Regal Zion needed defending.

'He's a circus horse, Jordan. A loved circus horse. He's my family.'

Jordan looked as though he was about to laugh again, but caught her eye and stopped.

She swallowed hard. 'Today I have found a family member I thought I'd never see again. I thought he was dead.' Her voice caught and Jordan studied her without saying a word. When he slowly nodded and turned back to help Bruce pack up the medical supplies, she knew the enormity of today's reunion and what it meant to her had begun to sink in. Maybe the guy had a heart after all.

Regal Zion let out a whinny and Starre wrapped her arms tight around his neck. 'I'm never letting you out of my sight again, boy.' *And I'm not going to tell Prince I've found you, either. He dared to sell you to buy himself a motorbike. He doesn't deserve a second chance!*

True, Prince was now a devoted husband and father, but selling Regal Zion and abandoning his own baby daughter fifteen years ago was something Starre could never forgive. Despite being an independent young woman, she felt like that devastated teenager again, trying to comprehend that the bottom had just fallen out of her world.

Chapter Two

Sky Clements didn't know what to feel. She should have felt abandoned and rejected like she had most of her life, but as she watched her birth mother struggle for breath, all she felt was intense sadness. Carrie Oldfield had once been pretty, according to Uncle Blaze, but there was no evidence of that left in the woman lying weakly on the hospital bed. Years of alcoholism had drained the life from her. Each breath made an eerie crackling noise as though something was broken.

She reached a hand to Sky and her blue eyes glistened. 'You're a pretty young thing, aren't you? How old are you now?'

Sky hesitantly took the woman's hand. The skin felt thin, as though it might tear at any moment. 'Fifteen.'

The woman nodded. 'Of course.' She squeezed her eyes shut for a moment. 'I have a lot of memory blanks these days, but I remember the day you were born. I always will.'

The woman's glazed eyes moved slowly to Blaze, who stood behind Sky. Even moving her eyes looked like an effort. Her skin was waxy and yellow. 'I know you hated me for what I did, Blaze. And you were so angry with Prince. But don't hold it against him. We had no choice. Tell Starre that, would you? Chase had no choice, either.'

'Chase?' Blaze had stepped forward and he looked perplexed. 'What does Chase have to do with anything?'

His arm came about Sky as he waited for Carrie to answer. Sky leaned into his chest, taking security from his presence. Carrie came close to a smile as her eyes rested on Blaze's arm about Sky, then came back to Sky herself. 'See, I did the right thing by you, didn't I?' She wheezed, then drew in a deep breath. 'Imagine having me as your mother.'

Sky swallowed the lump in her throat. 'You are my mother,' she whispered.

Carrie waved a thin hand toward Bonnie who stood behind Sky on the other side. 'No, love. She is your mother. You won't miss me when I'm gone and you shouldn't. This woman has been your mother since you were little.'

Sky felt the tears prick her eyes and tried to swallow against the tightness in her throat. She had never faced death before. It was overwhelming. She shook her head. 'I always wanted to meet you. Why wouldn't you let me before?'

Carrie barked out a cough before trying to lean up on her elbows. Blaze stepped forward to settle a pillow under her back. She lay back against it.

'Because Blaze and Bonnie are your family. I couldn't be a mother, Sky. I knew that.'

'But I could still have known you.'

'I wouldn't have been a good influence. I've done some bad things. You don't want to be like me.'

Sky frowned. What was she talking about?

The woman sank bank into her pillow, her strength obviously spent. 'I don't want you coming back, okay? This is goodbye. I'm ready to go and have instructed the doctors to let me. I'm tired of fighting.' She sucked in some deep breaths, gathering her strength again. 'I just wanted to see you one last time. Dying makes a person think back on life and I have a lot of regrets. But I don't regret leaving you with Blaze and Bonnie.' Her eyes were still closed but she moved her head in the direction of Blaze. 'Thank you, Blaze. Tell Starre I'm sorry and don't blame Chase.'

Both Blaze and Sky stepped forward and Sky tried to put her arms around her birth mother, but she didn't move. The crackled breathing had stopped. Her eyes flew to Blaze. 'Is she …?'

Blaze bit his lip, then leaned over Carrie, his ear close to her mouth. Then he pressed the emergency buzzer on the wall. Nurses came flying in. Sky stepped back, overwhelmed.

Slowly, in practiced rhythm, the group of doctors and nurses surrounding the bed moved back. A doctor turned to look at Blaze.

'I'm sorry. She's gone.'

Sky blinked rapidly. The doctor glanced to Sky. 'You're her daughter?'

She could only nod, her heart too much in turmoil to form any words. He rested a hand on her shoulder. 'She was waiting for you.'

'But I only just met her.'

The doctor nodded. 'She was waiting to say goodbye, to clear the air.'

Sky couldn't answer but she wanted to yell. *Clear the air? She only made me more confused than I ever was! Who is Chase? What's Aunty Starre got to do with all this? I don't even remember her. And why couldn't my real parents love me? What's so wrong with me?*

She turned and great rasping cries broke free from her heart and into the small hospital room. She was aware of Uncle Blaze and Bonnie wrapping her tightly in their arms, easing the pain through their embrace and unconditional love. She felt tears drip onto her bare arms and knew they were sharing her sorrow.

The trip home was subdued, but Sky had so many questions she couldn't keep them bottled up.

'Who is Chase?'

Uncle Blaze glanced back at her in the rear view mirror and she noticed the way his hand tightened on Bonnie's across the centre console of the car. 'He was the son of Marcos.'

'The circus owner? The one who tried to steal your horses when you were my age?' She'd heard the story many times. Uncle Blaze and his siblings, including her father, had been performers in Marcos' circus, but they had had a falling out. Things had turned nasty once Marcos lost his best performers.

'Yes. But Chase was different. He wasn't like his dad.'

'So what was my mother talking about? What happened with him and Aunty Starre?'

Blaze sighed. 'To tell you the truth, I don't know. Starre was kidnapped by Marcos at one stage and taken back to the circus. She would never tell me what happened. Not totally. But she changed when we left the circus.'

'And you left the circus because Granddad wanted you to get a good education and the circus people were upset about your belief in God?'

She noticed the way Blaze hesitated before he nodded. There was something he wasn't telling her. She pressed further. 'When did you find out about me?'

Blaze smiled. 'It was that day. The day Starre was kidnapped.'

Bonnie nodded and turned back to smile at Sky. 'I remember that day. He came charging over to my place, wanting to fight for you, protect you and love you.' She threw Blaze a tender look. 'It was one of the first things I loved about him.'

Sky grinned, her romantic heart softening. 'So I was part of what brought you together.'

Bonnie and Blaze both laughed at once. 'I guess you could say that.'

'So you are my parents and all is right with the world.'

The silence after her comment was so loud it jarred her. She saw the look that passed between them. What weren't they saying? It wasn't like them to be secretive. They were always completely open, reassuring her she was their child, an important part of their family.

Blaze cleared his throat. 'We've heard from your father again, Sky.'

'You're my father, Uncle Blaze.' She hadn't meant to snap the words but they came out before she could stop them. Prince was merely the man who had slept with Carrie. That was all. She had his genes, but God had created her and given her Blaze and Bonnie as parents.

Blaze didn't seem deterred by her reaction. His eyes remained on the road. 'We told him about you wanting a horse. He wants to give you one.'

Sky frowned. Prince hadn't bothered to visit her for ten years. He hadn't kept his promise to take her into his family when she was four, and he thought giving her a horse would make up for it?

She sat up straighter, tossing her long, dark hair over her shoulder. 'Can you please tell him no thank you?'

'Sky …'

She cut her mother off with a shake of her head. 'I don't want to think about it. Not now. My birth mother has just died.'

Bonnie simply nodded and reached a hand back in the car to rest it momentarily on Sky's arm. Tears formed in her eyes. She was so grateful God had given her Bonnie and Blaze. But nothing could take away the ache deep inside reminding her that her birth parents hadn't wanted her.

Chapter Three

Starre followed the numbers on the piece of paper in front of her, jabbing them into her phone. If she could talk to the woman who was supposed to be looking after Regal Zion she might be able to make some kind of case against the owner. She would do whatever it took to keep the horse. Despite the owner's accident he should have been making sure his partner looked after him. He should have been checking up. He would have if he was responsible and really cared.

'Yo. Courtney here.'

Starre was taken aback by the informal tone but pulled herself together. 'Hello, Courtney. Starre here from Animal Rescue. We have taken Regal Zion to our shelter but we need to speak to his owner.'

'What for?' The informal, friendly tone was gone.

'Neglecting an animal is a criminal offence and we need to establish the circumstances behind Regal Zion's condition.'

Courtney let out a huff of breath. 'Can't you just take him or something? Keep him and forget about it?'

'I'm sorry, but no. I have a few questions for you.'

'For me?' Her voice sounded panicked. 'I'm not the owner. Look, Mark got shot, okay? He was on duty that night … he's a policeman and decided to be a hero. He got shot in the leg and bashed. He was in a coma for a bit and I didn't know what to do with the horse.'

Starre tried to follow the rushed words. 'And he is now

in rehab?'

'Yes. Hey, what did you say your name was again?'

'Starre.'

'Starre, I'll text you all the details of the rehab centre. You can ask him all the questions you want. I know he looked after that horse, though. He loves him like ...' She paused and a sour note came to her voice. 'Well, like he should love me!'

Starre bit her lip, hearing the resentment in Courtney's tone. She wasn't sure she wanted to get wrapped up in all of this, but she needed to meet Regal Zion's owner. The horse's future and her happiness depended on it.

'Okay, thank you. That would be helpful.'

It was only a few minutes later a text came through. Starre looked at her screen and noted the details. She would ring the centre and arrange to meet Mark. Mark who? She had forgotten to get his last name but figured there couldn't be too many policemen in the one centre who were recovering from being shot.

She moved back to Regal Zion and inspected his legs. He whinnied and snorted, blowing her hair across her eyes. Laughing, she reached her arms up around his neck and hugged him.

Her mobile phone rang. She glanced at the screen. Blaze. He still tried calling her every week. Sometimes she answered but most of the time she ignored him. Should she tell him about Regal Zion? She still hadn't decided when she flipped her thumb across the green answer icon.

'Starre, how are you?' Blaze sounded cheerful as he always did.

'Good, Blaze. I got the email with the pics of Sky. She's doing well.'

'She is.' Starre could picture the look of pride on Blaze's face. She stopped herself rolling her eyes. That girl had to be the most spoiled, doted on teenager in the world. Every week she received more emails with pictures of Sky's smiling face as she received another trophy or award. The girl's eyes positively sparkled.

Blaze was continuing. 'But she's had a rough week. Carrie died.'

'Carrie?' Even as she questioned, Starre knew exactly who Blaze was talking about. Carrie Oldfield. Daughter of the elephant trainer. Seductress. Sky's mother. The woman who'd ruined her life.

'Yes. And she gave me a message for you.'

Starre had been stroking Regal Zion's nose as she spoke, but now she stiffened and paid full attention to Blaze.

'She said to tell you she's sorry and not to blame Chase. She said he had no choice.'

Starre couldn't answer. Her head swam and she sank to the ground and sat cross-legged, the phone still against her ear.

'Starre?'

Blaze sounded worried. She managed to clear her throat but still didn't answer. Blaze's voice came back now, more gently. 'What really happened that day you were kidnapped by Marcos?'

What happened? He was asking her the details now? He hadn't taken the time to listen that day. He had just told her how stupid she was to go back to the circus. It had taken a while to get through to him that she hadn't gone of her own free will. Then when she'd dropped the bombshell about Carrie being pregnant, no one asked anything else about what had happened to her. She didn't want to tell him now. Too many years had passed. She licked her dry lips. 'Why?'

'Because I'm guessing more is going on here than I ever knew.'

She let out a hard chuckle. 'It's not your worry now, Blaze. I am an independent adult. And you have your family to worry about. You worry about Bonnie and Sky. I can look after myself.'

Blaze didn't answer and she knew her dismissal had hurt him. Finally, his voice came back through her phone. 'Okay, but if you want to talk I'm here. I'm praying for you.'

'I know.'

'I love you, Starre.'

'I know. Bye.'

Slowly, she pressed the screen on her phone to end the call. It had been fifteen years now. Why could she still not tell Blaze she loved him, too? Why did the word 'love' die on her lips and leave a bitter taste in her mouth? And what did Carrie mean that Chase had no choice? She shrugged. Carrie was gone so now she would never know.

She left Regal Zion and began the rounds of cleaning out the animal cages. She moved slowly, her mind refusing to ignore the past any longer.

Digby, the abandoned Australian cattle dog, seemed to sense her mood and licked at her hand, whining. She forced herself to look at him and rubbed his ears. He rolled onto his stomach and wagged his tail playfully.

'I know, Digby. I'm not paying attention, am I?' She rubbed his tummy absently, before looking into his grey eyes. Grey eyes like Chase's eyes. She squatted beside Digby but squeezed her eyes shut. 'Oh Chase, what did Carrie mean?'

She hadn't let herself think of Chase for years. She had loved the circus owner's son since she was a little girl. She had admired the older boy and had felt special every time he paid her attention. From the day he'd rescued her from the snake's enclosure. Clay and Carrie had lured her in and locked the door, knowing her phobia. Chase found her cowering in the corner, hands over her ears, eyes shut tight and trembling. He had lifted her up, stepping over the large python lying between her and the door, and carried her outside. The older boy had let her cling to him until she stopped trembling and then had gone to tell his younger brother and Carrie exactly what he thought of their cruel prank.

And he'd taught her how to handle the snakes. She had only been six years old, but from that day she followed him everywhere and he seemed to enjoy her attention.

As she grew older, she sensed that he admired her in return. And then one day he told her what a beautiful young woman she'd become and kissed her. Her world changed that day. He loved her.

Or so I thought. How could I have been so stupid? She shook her head, trying to get the image of his grey eyes from her mind, and his smile; the way he looked at her.

Digby jumped up from the ground and Starre stood. Enough of the past. Time to go and meet Regal Zion's new owner.

'Sorry, Digby. I've got work to do.' She gave the dog one last pat and left, gazing into the distance, wondering whether Regal Zion would be hers by the time the sun sank behind the hills that evening.

A woman stood at the information desk, smiling warmly at Starre. 'Can I help you?'

'Yes. I'm from Animal Rescue. A young woman by the name of Courtney Panton directed me here to speak to her partner in regard to his horse. She said he is a policeman. He was shot on duty.'

The woman nodded and pointed down the hall. 'Turn left into the trauma recovery unit and you will find him in room four. The physiotherapist should have finished working with him for today.'

'Thanks.' Starre turned and headed down the hall, her work boots making a clacking rhythm on the polished floors. Maybe she should have dressed up? No, she looked more official in her Animal Rescue uniform.

She knocked gently on the door of room four and poked her head around the corner. She could already hear a woman's raised voice but didn't think to stop in time. She recognised Courtney's voice from the phone.

'I *did* look after your stupid horse, Mark. I don't know how to rub it down and ride it and all that stuff you spend so much time doing. Geez, that horse is higher maintenance than I am!'

A quiet, calm voice responded. 'Courte, we've been over this so many times. All I asked was for you to make sure he was okay. I don't think being caught in barbed wire for two days is okay, do you?'

Courtney spun around and caught sight of Starre, but didn't

stop. 'I don't know, Mark,' she shot back over her shoulder. 'You should know. But you survived being shot and mangled, didn't you?'

'Yes, I did.' His voice was still deep and calm.

'Well, maybe I haven't survived it, have you thought of that? You and your humility, refusing to be interviewed by the papers, refusing to be labelled a hero.'

'I'm not a hero. I was doing my job.'

'Yes, and your job is going to get you killed. I just don't know if I can sit around waiting for that to happen.'

'Courte?' His voice was pleading, but Courtney threw a disgusted look at him over her shoulder. 'Don't worry, Marko. The rescue woman is here. Maybe she can rescue our relationship too.'

Starre flinched at the harshness in the woman's voice as she flounced from the room without another word. Helplessly, Starre found her eyes drawn to the young man standing beside the bed. A neat beard covered his chin, but above it to the left of his face, deep, ragged scars ran from his cheek to his ear. His hands rested on a walking frame and he used it to move forward, an obvious limp in his left leg. He wore shorts and his right leg was well toned. His left one looked thin and weak.

'Starre.'

Her eyes flew to his as he said her name. His voice came out husky and regret filled her that she had witnessed his partner's verbal attack. He must be in turmoil right now.

'Sorry, I can come back later.' She forced her eyes to meet his. They were troubled eyes. Grey and full of pain.

'No.' He made a sudden move forward, then stopped again. 'Starre, I can't believe it's you.'

She frowned. Did she know this man? He raised a hand to his scar and she saw it was shaking. Her eyes flew back to his eyes. They were familiar, but ...

'Do I know you?'

He smiled then. A tentative, half-smile that somehow

touched her heart. 'Mark is my nickname. Short for Marcos. Chase Marcos.'

Starre's breath caught in her throat and she had a coughing fit. 'Chase?' The word came out in a squeak.

He smiled a full smile and she knew it truly was him despite the scar covering half his face. He looked so much younger when he smiled.

'It's been a long time.' He still looked uncertain and she didn't know what to say.

He looked at her clipboard. 'Obviously we have official business to do, but there are so many more personal things we need to talk about.'

It was all too overwhelming. It was as though her past had pushed itself into her present these last few days and she simply couldn't ignore it any longer. Chase was right. She had so many questions, so many hurts that had never been resolved.

She raised the clipboard. 'Should we do this first?'

He nodded and lowered himself into the chair beside his bed, indicating another one nearby. 'Pull up a chair. Sorry I can't do it for you.'

She dragged it over, wondering at how her heart beat faster every step she took toward him. She couldn't keep her eyes off him.

He was looking at her as though he thought she would suddenly disappear. She tried not to look at his scar and instead focussed on his eyes. Still open and friendly. She wished he wouldn't look at her that way. Didn't he realise how much he had hurt her?

'So, Regal Zion is yours.'

He nodded.

'I need your full name and date of birth.'

He gave a sideways grin. 'They haven't changed since last time you saw me.'

He knew she would remember? She hoped he wouldn't notice the warmth creeping into her face as she jotted them down.

'Occupation?'

'Policeman.'

She stared at him. 'Why?'

He leaned toward her, trying to see the form she was writing on. 'That question's not on there, is it?'

She bit her lip. 'No. I was just wondering.' His fair head was close enough that she could see he also had a bald patch on his head around another deep scar. Her eyes slid shut. What had he suffered? No matter how much he had hurt her she would never wish this on him!

He looked up and his eyes twinkled at her. 'Personal questions later. Let's do this form first.'

Anyone would think he still had feelings for her, the way he was looking at her. Did he think she would choose to go through that again? She forced away the feelings he was inciting and focussed on business. 'When did you acquire Regal Zion and from whom?'

He didn't answer until she looked up from the form and met his grey eyes again. 'Fourteen years ago from Prince Clements.'

'But—'

He lifted a finger with a smile and pointed to the paper resting on her lap. 'Official business first, then personal questions later, remember? I promise I will explain everything.'

She managed to drag her eyes away from him and focus back on the paper. His smile still had the same effect on her, even after all these years. 'Okay. Next question. Who is his vet?'

Chase gave the name and from there the questions and answers came smoothly. It was clear Chase had all the right answers. He had looked after Regal Zion well.

Then came the tough questions. Starre tried to remain official. 'Are you aware that Regal Zion came to us in an emaciated state, dehydrated and badly injured by the barbed wire wrapped around his legs?'

She looked up when there was no answer and saw the colour

had drained from his face. 'I am aware.'

She waited for him to say more. He sighed. 'I was injured in the course of my work and was in a coma for several days. This can be verified by my doctor and also by my boss if you need it official. As soon as I was able to think clearly again I asked Courtney to check up on Regal Zion for me. She said she would but she's not very fond of horses. She told me he was doing fine. I couldn't check myself.'

The remorse in his expression left no doubt he was telling the truth. Starre jotted down notes, then laid down her clipboard. She looked into his eyes. 'I'm sorry, Chase.'

His eyes widened. 'What do you mean *you're* sorry?' I've been wanting to apologise for years and here you are telling me you're sorry?'

'I'm sorry for all you've been through.'

'Oh.'

She bit her lip, just looking at him. Where to start? And what if the answers to her questions just caused more confusion and hurt? She needed a safe question to begin with.

'It's okay.' His voice and tone were gentle. He took the clipboard from her hands and lay it on the bed. 'Talk to me.'

Surprised by the sting of tears threatening in her eyes, she took a deep breath. 'So you bought Regal Zion?'

He nodded. 'I heard Dad speaking to a guy he got to do his dirty work sometimes. Guy Theile. He was going to pay Guy to buy Regal in his name, on his behalf. He knew Prince would never want Regal Zion back in the circus. So he set Guy up with a wonderful story about his special needs son who needed a horse for therapy.'

Starre's eyes widened. Marcos was so deceitful. 'So how did *you* end up with him?'

'Offered to pay Guy more to get him for me instead.'

Starre's brows shot up and Chase looked away. 'I know.

I wasn't honest either. But I guess I just wanted to see justice done for a change. And I thought Prince might want to buy him back one day.'

'You offered him back?'

Chase moved his injured leg, still not meeting her eyes. 'It was the plan, but after I'd had Regal Zion for a year, I couldn't part with him.' He looked up, his brow furrowed. 'I guess I couldn't understand how Prince could have sold him, and if he did it once …'

Starre nodded. She had never been able to understand that either.

'So did your dad find out?'

'Not until later when Guy told him. I never returned to the circus after that day. I just left with the horse trailer I'd bought, went to Goulburn, bought a property just out of town with enough room for a horse and signed up for the police force. It was the final straw for me. I was so sick of Dad's games. He was playing with people's lives! Especially your family's. He had betrayed me so often but he accused me of the ultimate betrayal once I became a policeman.'

Starre nodded, imagining how angry Marcos would have been. He insisted police didn't belong in the lives of circus people. But in the meantime he had set himself up as a dictator, running and manipulating the lives of everyone in the circus.

'So why a policeman?'

Chase shrugged. 'Someone has to stop people like my dad. You can't treat people like that.'

Starre remembered back to the day Chase had rescued her from the snake enclosure. Chase liked justice. He'd told her once that life wasn't fair, but he believed justice was always carried out somehow, either here or in the afterlife. She studied his battered face. Were his injuries justice for the way he'd hurt her so many years ago?

No, God. I didn't ask for justice. You'd better not have done that on my behalf!

Suddenly forgiveness seemed a whole lot more attractive than justice. And yet she had been carrying around her burden of hurt for so many years. She hadn't forgiven him and now she desperately needed to. But she still didn't understand.

She started as he reached long fingers and smoothed the furrow in her brow. 'What are you thinking?'

Suddenly her throat was too tight to speak. Tears formed in the corner of her eyes. He squeezed her hand. 'What happened between us, Starre?'

What happened? He knew what had happened! Sudden anger hit her as heat shot through her body. She stood abruptly and spoke between clenched teeth. 'Nothing happened, remember? What happened was between you and Carrie.' She shook her head. 'I loved you, Chase. You knew I loved you. It wasn't just some crazy infatuation of a needy little girl.'

'Hey, it's okay.'

He tried to reach for her, but she stepped back. 'It's not okay. It's never been okay.'

He stood and took an unsteady step forward, and before she knew it, she was in his arms, sobbing against his chest, feeling his cool cotton shirt becoming damp with her tears.

'Sh.' His hands were stroking her hair, holding her against him. 'I promise it's all going to be all right.'

She felt special, protected, just like old times. But there was still one raging question. She needed to know.

'Let me tell you about Sky.' His deep, calm voice reassured her that he would explain it all.

Chapter Four

Sky rolled over on her bed and strained to hear Blaze and Bonnie talking.

'I think we should tell Prince about Carrie.' Blaze's calm voice of reason wafted through the doorway.

'What good would it do? Prince has had nothing to do with her for fifteen years! It would only cause unnecessary regret.'

Regret. Such a mild word for what he should be feeling. Sky kicked her pillow off the bed but it didn't make her feel better.

She heard Blaze's voice again. 'Bonnie, is this about your fears?'

Sky lifted herself to her elbows. What fears could her foster mother have? The hint of panic in Bonnie's tone might have suggested she was afraid. But of what?

'I don't know, to tell you the truth.' Bonnie's voice caught and Sky knew Blaze would be taking her into his arms to comfort her. Why couldn't she have been their real daughter? Why did God have to let her be born to a mother and father who didn't really want her, who didn't love and support one another and never even thought of commitment?

With a sigh, she went to her computer and jiggled the mouse to wake up the screen. Fifty-four likes already. She had only posted the picture of herself doing acrobatic diving half an hour ago. She wondered if Prince would notice it and be proud of her. Even Blaze and Bonnie said she had his talent and mannerisms.

She had his smooth, flowing walk; like a dance, his dazzling smile and heart-melting eyes.

But she refused to use her physical attributes to seduce anyone the way he had. In fact, she was determined never to kiss a guy until she was sure she wanted to marry him. He had to be someone special. And she would wait until she was at least sixteen. She wouldn't be like her father who got a girl pregnant at sixteen and then abandoned her.

Her computer made a noise. An email. She clicked her email icon and smiled. Jake. When was he going to get up to date and join Facebook?

'Final Camp details.' She scanned his email. Some foster children were going to be at the youth camp and he wanted to make sure she understood they could be a bit difficult. They would be in her cabin.

Thanks, Jake. She smiled despite herself. It was a compliment that Jake felt he could entrust her with them.

'*I heard about your biological mum,*' he had typed. '*I've been praying for you. Don't feel obligated to come. It's okay if you need time.*'

Was he kidding? This camp was exactly what she needed. It would re-centre her, remind her she was loved by God and others. Going to a Christian school helped with that, but there was something special about being at camps, away from the comforts of home and completely focussed on God and loving other people. Caring for the girls from the foster home would help her forget her own pain for a while.

'Thanks Jake, but I'm doing okay.' She spoke the words out loud as she typed them. Jake had clearly never seen her Facebook page, but he loved and respected her as much as she loved and respected him. 'Can't wait to catch up again.'

How to end? It was always a problem when she wrote to him. Facebook was a lot more casual than email. You could just make a comment here and there and not really address the person you were talking to. But email was more like a letter. Jake always signed off, 'Blessings, Jake.'

She didn't want to copy him, but she didn't know what to put. 'Love' was a word she didn't want to throw about too freely. 'Kind regards' was too formal. 'Your sister in Christ' sounded like she was trying to be spiritual.

She pictured Jake. His plain features and ginger hair made him nothing special to look at, but her respect for him went deep. He had charisma, just as Bonnie had said the first time she met him. He was an excellent camp leader and seemed to sense whenever someone was troubled or needing encouragement.

'He's mature for his age,' Blaze had commented after meeting him at the end of the last camp when he came to collect Sky. 'I chatted with him for a while. His Bible knowledge is amazing for someone so young.'

Suddenly Sky felt the need to see his face. She clicked back onto Facebook and typed in 'Camp Oaken'. She scrolled through pictures until she came to one of him. His head was thrown back as he laughed and Sky couldn't help smiling. It would be good to see him again.

'Please God, encourage him, bless him and use him at this camp. Grant him his deepest desires.'

She clicked back onto her email and finished it, 'Love and prayers, Sky.'

***

Jake read Sky's email, then let his head fall into his hands. She was still coming to camp. He had thought the death of her biological mother was God's way of keeping her away. What was he going to do? He stood and paced the room before charging out the door. She had to be told. He had to make his parents understand.

They were in the kitchen, working through the camp freezer,

checking the dates on the frozen foods.

'Mum, Dad, we have to tell Sky. She needs to know who's coming.'

He knew he sounded officious, but they had to understand. Marion lifted her head and studied him before Charles did the same.

'Does she even know we might have new camp workers coming?'

Jake tried to remember. Had he told her? He had shared with her that the camp would need to fold if they didn't increase the number of camps and get up to scratch with the new regulations.

'I don't think so. But still, she needs to be told.'

Marion bit her lip. 'I don't think that's a good idea.'

'But they're coming on Thursday and she'll be here. She's been so hurt. Imagine how betrayed she'll feel.'

Marion shut the freezer and leaned back against it. 'Jake, you know what will happen if we tell her.'

Yes, he knew. She would refuse to come.

'He specifically asked us not to say anything, Jake.' His father's eyes were searching his. 'I don't necessarily agree with that but we need to respect his wishes.'

'Respect *his* wishes? What about Sky's wishes? We know what hers would be. She wouldn't come anywhere near here.'

Charles nodded. 'But maybe she needs to. Maybe this needs to be sorted out once and for all. Sky has issues with forgiveness. Maybe God wants to do something special this camp.'

Jake let out a deep sigh. He remembered the day Sky had confided her deepest pain to him. Her normally bright eyes had been filled with tears as she spilled her heart, telling him about her real parents.

'They abandoned me, Jake. If my own parents can't love me, how can I expect anyone else to?'

His heart had constricted as he looked into her beautiful eyes. *I love you!* his mind had screamed, but instead of voicing it, he had enfolded her in his arms. 'God loves you, Sky. More than you could ever imagine. I will pray you begin to understand the beauty of adoption. Then you will understand just how loved you really are.'

She had shaken her head. 'I feel so rejected.'

He had sat back, unable to believe what he was hearing. The stunningly beautiful and popular Sky Clements felt rejected? Wasn't it enough that the rest of the world admired and loved her?

Clearly not. *Lord, help her understand your love and forgiveness. And help me be the friend she needs when all I want to do is claim her as my own to love and cherish for always. Give me patience and self-control. Let me see her for who she truly is.*

She had looked up at him then, her eyes suddenly darkening as she pushed back from him. 'Sorry, Jake. I didn't mean to be all clingy and needy.'

The independent, together Sky was back. Regret knifed through him as she stood with a lopsided smile and stepped back. 'Thanks for listening.'

'No worries. I'll be praying for you.'

She nodded, then took another step backwards, confusion flashing through her eyes before she headed back to her cabin.

It had been a breakthrough moment. Sky had seemed to realise he wasn't trying to make her fall in love with him. That set him apart from all the other guys her age at the camp and allowed a deep friendship to develop. And he no longer felt nervous around her. She was stunningly beautiful, but she had needs and hurts just like any other human who needed to understand God's love.

CHAPTER FIVE

Starre bit the inside of her cheek as Chase leaned his elbows on his knees. His voice was deep, filled with regret.

'When Dad found out Carrie was pregnant he thought he would use it to his advantage the way he does with everything. He knew you guys were leaving and he wanted a Clements child to be part of the future of the circus. He thought you guys would take the baby and Carrie with you if you knew Prince was the father, so he supplied Carrie with more alcohol on the proviso she said the baby was mine.'

Starre gasped in horror. 'And you went along with it?' She knew she sounded accusatory, but she simply couldn't help it.

'I was going to lose you anyway, Starre.'

Starre threw herself and the chair backwards, not able to be anywhere near him at that moment.

'Starre?' There was pleading in his tone. 'I'm sorry. There's no excuse for it but I was young and stupid and still wanted to please my father. I've lived every day of my life trying to make up for it.'

'What do you mean?' Her words came out in a whisper, but he must have heard.

'I took on this job. I fight for truth and justice. I …' He swallowed hard. 'I got shot rescuing a little girl and boy from a home full of ice addicts. The sergeant got them out while I took the fallout.'

Starre let out a little cry. She felt overwhelmed. She needed a moment. Without a word she stood and left the room. The hallway was empty. She began to pace, her work boots making a loud clack on the floor with each step.

She had left the circus believing Chase loved Carrie; that he had betrayed her. She had tried to put them far from her mind, but everything had changed the day Clive and Banksie grabbed her at the school gate and forced her into the truck, taking her back to the circus.

Chase had met her at the gate, his eyes sad. 'Starre. We need to clear something up.'

She had struggled to get out of Clive's grasp and Chase had nodded at him. 'Let her go. She needs to see what I have to show her.'

He had tried to take her hand but she shook him off. Still, she followed him into Carrie's caravan. Before she reached the door she could hear it; the pathetic wail of a tiny baby. She stopped. Why did he want her to see his and Carrie's baby? It would break her heart.

He looked back at her and reached a hand. 'Come on, Starre. I have to show you. You won't believe me unless I do.'

Curiosity got the better of her and she felt the caravan sink with each weighted step behind Chase. The place was a complete mess. The baby lay on a blanket on the floor, used bottles haphazardly left around. Chase was speaking to the baby and Starre moved closer. The wailing stopped and the baby smiled. Its dark eyes sparkled with joy and its perfect little mouth lifted up into a familiar smile. Too familiar. This baby looked just like her.

'What?'

Chase turned back to her, lifting the baby into his arms. 'This is Sky Clements, your niece. Prince and Carrie's daughter.'

Starre took a hurried step back, pain like a knife stabbing her chest. 'Carrie was sleeping with both of you?'

Chase shook his head and the baby reached and grabbed his shirt with her tiny fists. 'No. There was never anything between Carrie and me.'

'Is this some kind of cruel game?' Starre's voice came out in a high pitched screech.

'No, it's no game, I promise you.' Chase lowered baby Sky back to the blanket. She didn't miss the baby's smile that seemed to mock her. The little girl adored Chase. The way she had.

'You promise me?' Tears filled her eyes.

His hand reached to touch her face and she lost it. 'You told me I was beautiful. You kissed me. Then two days later you told me you were Sky's father. Now you say you're not and my brother is?' She began beating her fists against his chest, crying helplessly.

The caravan moved and she knew someone else had joined them. Someone grabbed her wrists to stop her assault on Chase and she looked up into the face of his father, Marcos. 'Starre, I can't have your family, so I want your horses. Got it? I know you love your precious family and you would hate to see anything happen to that religious brother of yours.'

Her eyes widened as she registered his threat on Blaze's life. He let go of her wrists and took some rolled up papers from his top pocket. He shoved them into her chest. 'Being beautiful can't get you everything you want.' He smirked. 'But playing dirty can and I'm an expert at that. So either you return to the circus or you get these papers signed and hand those horses over. If you don't, you'll regret it the rest of your life.' He let out a vicious chuckle. 'Blaze won't though, because he won't have a life to regret.'

Starre stared at him before spinning toward Chase, letting loose a flying kick that got him in the face. He fell backward and the baby screwed up its pretty little face and started to scream. She turned on Marcos, but he was ready. He grabbed both of her wrists in an iron grip and shoved her toward the door.

'None of that, missie. You've got some serious thinking to do before your precious family come and collect you. And you can tell them you miss the circus so much you just came back for a visit, okay?'

Starre stared at him defiantly, but she knew she was trapped. She had been tricked. She would never love or allow herself to be loved again.

Starre wasn't aware she was now sitting down against the wall of the rehabilitation centre, crying her heart out until she felt an arm come around her. Startled, she looked up to see that Chase had lowered himself down beside her. His walker stood beside him and his long legs stretched out in front of him.

'I'm so sorry. I underestimated the strength of your feelings for me. I underestimated my father's hold over me. I've tried to make it right my whole life, but I know I can't make it right with you.'

Starre gulped back her tears. 'So there was never anything going on between you and Carrie?'

'No.'

'I still don't understand. I thought you had feelings for me. You kissed me and then just a few days later you told me Carrie was expecting your baby.' Then it struck her. Marcos was behind the kiss too. Marcos thought she might convince her family to stay if she was seduced by Chase.

'Your father told you to kiss me, didn't he?' Her voice was low, resigned.

A faraway look came to his eyes and she knew she'd hit the nail on the head. His eyes darkened and she knew he was remembering it as clearly as she was.

'The whole thing was a mess, Starre. Dad thought having Sky in the circus would be the answer to everything. But he hadn't counted on Carrie getting so badly into the alcohol and not coping. He told me to look after her.'

'But he hadn't counted on Blaze contacting Department of Families and taking Sky either, had he?'

Chase shook his head and she remembered the way he'd tenderly held Sky that day she'd been introduced. Sky hadn't even been his, but he'd loved her. She felt tears stinging her eyes. 'Chase, I attacked you in front of her. I was vicious.'

One side of his mouth turned up in a sad smile. 'I deserved it. But it was the last time I let my dad tell me what to do.'

They were interrupted as a doctor strode down the hall, stethoscope slung around his neck. He stopped at the sight of Chase on the floor beside Starre. 'Chase, are you okay?'

He looked up at the doctor with a lopsided grin. 'Yeah, but I wouldn't mind a hand up.'

The doctor grinned in return, reaching his hand to grasp Chase's and pull him up. He helped him stand, then placed his walker in front of him. Starre stood too, unable to keep her eyes off him. He began the slow walk back to his room and she walked by his side.

'So what now?' she asked.

'I'm not sure. I may not be able to return to work in the same capacity. I might be paper chasing the rest of my life.' He looked down at his leg. 'It all depends how well the nerves in my leg heal.'

'What about you and Courtney?'

He let out a deep sigh. 'I honestly don't know. She's not happy with me right now and my new look has had a bit of an impact on her. She's not finding it easy and I understand that.'

Starre studied him. His scars were unmissable, but they couldn't detract from the depth of his grey eyes or the warmth of his heart and smile. 'You been together long?'

'Six months.' He stopped to catch his breath. 'How about you? Anyone special in your life?'

'Just Regal Zion.'

He stopped as though she'd slapped him. 'So you're taking him, then.'

She swallowed hard. 'I honestly don't know.'

He shook his head. 'Do what you need to do.' His eyes slid closed for a moment before he continued limping back toward his room. He stopped at the doorway. 'I need to rest, but I'd like to catch up some more.'

Starre nodded, uncertain. Should she hug him? Thank him? Yell at him and make him understand just how much he had hurt her? Or cling to him and never let go?

Instead she took a deep breath and just managed a simple, 'Bye then.'

She was nearly at the door when his voice stopped her. 'Starre?'

She turned back. He was holding her folder out to her. She raced forward to take it from his hand, but he held onto it. She raised questioning eyes to his. Slowly, he let go of the board.

'I wanted to kiss you. I wasn't just doing what my dad said. I … you were very special to me. I want you to know that.'

Overwhelmed, she simply nodded before racing out of the room and down the hallway in a walk much closer to a run. She needed to get back to Regal Zion; to hug him, and hold him tight while she still had him. There was no way she could keep him from Chase any longer than was necessary.

Chapter Six

Alexa looked down at the ground far below. She would never really do it, but the other foster girl cowering in the corner of the room didn't know that.

She narrowed her eyes. 'I'm going to count to ten, Joanna, and then I'm going to jump!' A glance showed her the eyes behind her were full of terror. The satisfaction that filled her both frightened and confused her. Power had never been at her disposal before when she'd threatened suicide. For the first time in her life she didn't feel helpless.

Hearing Joanna scramble to her feet from the corner of the room, she couldn't help just the hint of a smile. Yet she remained poised as though ready for action. She had to be believable.

'Rachel! Quick!' she heard Joanna's frightened voice scream through the house. 'Please, Rachel. You have to come!'

'Coming!' a musical voice called back, and soon a motherly woman with wispy blond hair surrounding her oval face stood in the room.

'She said she's going to kill herself again!' the pasty faced Joanna cried. 'She said she's going to jump out the window.'

'Alexa?' Rachel asked, her voice calm despite the concern showing clearly in her gentle brown eyes. Alexa moved forward slightly until she sat at the edge of the open window, her gaze focused on the ground two stories below.

'I mean it!' she said coldly. 'If you make me go to camp, I'll kill myself.'

Rachel's eyebrows raised in surprise but her voice remained gentle and serene. 'No one ever said you have to go, Alexa. We're not forcing you to. It's your choice.'

Alexa looked around in surprise. She was used to being bullied and pushed around by her father. Now she was using the same method to gain control in her own life but it seemed she didn't need to.

With a shrug, she swung her legs back from the window sill and came away from it. 'I don't want to go.'

'You don't?'

She looked to the door at the sound of Paul's deep voice and her heart softened. Her foster brother was studying her, disappointment etched across his smooth features. He must know she was infatuated with him, yet he always remained gentle and understanding, much like Rachel and Prince. She'd never met anyone like him.

She watched as her foster mother, Rachel, calmly squatted beside Joanna, drawing her into a hug and helping her up from the floor. Paul moved toward Alexa and she came away from the window to his side. The tension in the room evaporated and she suppressed a smile. Power was exhilarating.

'I don't want to leave the horses,' she said, aware her voice came out whiny, but needing to make them understand. Of course she also hated the idea of being away from Paul and of being shut up in a cabin with strangers. She often had nightmares and woke up in a cold sweat. She needed her space.

Paul's brown eyes were earnest as he smiled at her. 'If it helps, I'm going now too. I know I'm not a horse, but maybe having someone else you know will help.'

'Why are you going?'

'They needed more leaders.' His eyes were questioning

Rachel as he spoke.

Rachel took a deep breath. 'We're also planning to come mid-week, now. And some of our horses.'

'What?'

'The camp wants to introduce horses and we're looking into taking up a position there.'

'We might move there?'

Rachel nodded. 'If God directs us that way. Prince and I are praying about it.'

Alexa stared at Rachel a moment before relenting. 'Okay, I'll go.' She made herself sound unenthusiastic when the truth was she loved that idea. She turned back to her suitcase, then gave the girl nestled in Rachel's arms a look of reproach. 'Come on, Joanna. Help me pack.'

Now that the drama was over, Joanna seemed to gain courage and came to stand by her foster sister. Alexa sensed that though she was quiet, intense anger flowed from the girl. She tried to see the eyes Joanna so carefully kept down. 'Joanna?'

Joanna looked up and those usually fearful eyes blazed with an intimidating fury. Then just as quickly, it was gone. Alexa wondered if she had imagined it. Maybe she had pushed too far.

'Want me to help you pack too?' she offered, by way of apology.

Joanna simply nodded, handing Alexa the soap and toothpaste Rachel had put out for them.

Chapter Seven

In the quiet of her room, Sky was packing. She glanced around, taking in the comforts. She would miss them. She would miss her phone and computer the most. Camp rules stipulated they were to be left at home. She looked at her lacy curtains. She would miss them too, and the delicate lilac of her bedroom. Blaze and Bonnie had great taste. Her room was fit for a princess.

She thought of the foster girls. Would they have ever had nice things like she had? She looked at the curtains again, then moved to the window. Carefully balancing on her desk, she reached up and took them down. Her cabin was going to have a hint of luxury this year. Next, she moved to the beautiful wall hanging of a lion and a lamb lying peacefully on the grass, snuggled up together. A taste of heaven. Whatever those girls had been through, they needed a taste of heaven.

She heard the phone ring and Bonnie's voice as she answered it. Moments later, Bonnie stood in the doorway holding out the cordless phone and staring at the empty window and the blank space on the wall.

Sky merely grinned.

Bonnie looked back at the phone. 'Marion for you.' She handed the phone over. Marion was the camp manager and Sky loved her like another mother.

'Hi, Marion.'

'Sky! What are you up to?'

'I'm busy packing my suitcase. I've got half my room packed. Might need another few suitcases. I hope you don't charge for excess baggage.'

'Sky, don't!' Marion groaned, but Sky could tell she was amused.

'There's nothing to worry about. I won't bring Bruno and Lorice this year.'

The woman let out a laugh. 'You keep those pet mice at home, Sky Clements! You're too old to get away with smuggling little creatures into camp now.'

Sky grinned at the memory. It had been at the kids' camp she'd attended as a ten year old. Bruno and Lorice had enjoyed a grand adventure. They had ended up spending most of the week in the girls' toilets because the boys insisted on stealing them for practical jokes. However, even the girls' toilets hadn't been safe and Bruno and Lorice managed to have a few adventures in girls' sleeping bags.

'I still don't know how those horrible creatures of yours came out alive!' Marion said. Then she became serious. 'Sky, I know Jake already told you, but I just wanted to check in person. We've put you in charge of a small cabin this year, but it will be the most difficult. We have two girls coming from pretty awful backgrounds, and we thought you would be the best one to help them. Charles and I discussed it with Jake and we all agreed. They're from the same foster home, so we thought we'd keep them together. Alexa had an abusive father and Joanna's mother was murdered by her de-facto less than a year ago. Both are still struggling, but their foster parents thought camp is probably the best thing that can happen to them.'

Sky listened quietly. The more she understood about the girls, the more she could get to know them and help them.

'Jake said you lost your mother recently.' Marion's voice was husky with emotion as though she were sharing Sky's sorrow. No wonder Jake was the way he was. Marion was a special mother to have.

'Yes. But like I told Jake, I'm okay.'

'You let me or Charles … or Jake know if you're finding it difficult. We can always swap things around. And Sky?'

'Yes?'

'How are things with you and your real dad?'

Sky blew out a breath. 'I'm not really ready to think about it. I've just lost my mum.'

'Oh. Okay.' Marion seemed to hesitate and Sky frowned, waiting. But she didn't say anything except goodbye before she hung up.

Sky wandered slowly back to her room. Unzipping her suitcase, she added the items she'd previously decided not to take for the sake of being mature. It seemed these girls could do with a bit of fun in their lives.

She glanced around her bedroom one more time. Yes, she had everything. Her suitcase even contained the traditional hair dryer and iron that always had the girls at camp laughing over her insistence on living in comfort, whatever the location.

'Sky, did you get your swimmers from the clothes basket?'

Sky smiled as Bonnie popped her head in the door. 'Yes. How could I forget my swimmers, Mum?'

Diving was her forté. There were many and varied things she was good at, but diving was what she loved most. And now that she had a bikini she enjoyed showing off her athletic, toned body. It had taken her a long time to convince Bonnie to buy her a bikini, but finally she'd given in.

Bonnie grinned. 'You never know, Sky. You're not exactly rememberful.'

'Rememberful?' Sky gave her bubbly laugh. 'Is that the word you use when you can't remember the opposite to forgetful?'

'Is there an opposite to forgetful?' Bonnie challenged.

Sky shrugged, and the two laughed together as they began carrying suitcases downstairs to the waiting car.

As they headed to camp, Sky watched Bonnie, love filling her. She truly was blessed to have such an amazing mother, even if she wasn't her own. All that was missing from her life now was a horse.

Now seemed a good idea to bring the subject up again. 'Mum, there is a diving competition Sandra was telling me about. She thinks I could win it.'

Bonnie nodded. 'I'm sure you could, if Sandra thinks you can.'

Sky nodded. Sandra was an amazing coach and the older woman had quickly become her friend.

'There is a prize. It's twenty thousand dollars.'

Bonnie's eyes widened, but she waited for Sky to continue.

'Do you think if I won it, I could get myself a horse and use some of the rest of the money to pay for agistment?'

Bonnie didn't answer for a moment, then she took her eyes off the road to meet Sky's. 'Your dad would get you a horse.'

She shook her head. 'This is something I need to do on my own.' She forced her usual playful grin. 'Besides, there's a horse nearby who's pining for me. I sense it. It's living for the day it becomes mine. It's not some spoiled, well-bred creature. It's been rescued and needs adopting. It needs *me*. You wouldn't want to separate us forever, would you?'

Bonnie laughed. 'You're unbelievable, you know that? I think your father got the names for you and your sister mixed up.'

'What do you mean?' Prince hadn't even been around when she was born, let alone named. 'Blaze is the only real father I have.'

Bonnie chose to ignore the comment. 'Your half-sister—

'Philippa'. It means 'Lover of horses' or something like that.'

When Sky said nothing, Bonnie reached and put a hand on her shoulder. 'Sky, you know you could have lived amongst horses if you'd accepted your father's offer of adoption two years ago.'

Bonnie's face paled even as she said it, but Sky could feel her anger building. 'Why would I accept his offer of adoption? He's never even been to see me! He abandoned me.'

'You don't know the full story, Sky. He's accepted your decision to stay with us, but he's offered to give you a horse.'

'Why? To make up for not seeing me all these years? As much as I long for a horse, I could never accept one from him.'

Bonnie looked more upset, but Sky tried to shut it from her mind. 'Mum, I don't want my horse chosen by a man who is practically a stranger. I want to choose my own.'

She glanced at Bonnie and knew she'd noticed the way she called her 'mum'. Bonnie hadn't said anything but Sky knew refusing to be adopted by Blaze and Bonnie had been a source of pain to her.

Her shoulders sagged in defeat. She wasn't sure why she couldn't accept the offer. Maybe because her real parents hadn't wanted her. Somewhere deep down she was afraid that once she accepted, she would no longer be good enough. She couldn't bear the thought of being rejected again.

Bonnie rested a gentle hand on Sky's arm and her brilliant blue eyes seemed to look right through her and into her heart. 'I'm praying for you, my Sky.'

Sky didn't answer, and she determined never to bring up the subject of getting a horse again.

Chapter Eight

Starre picked up her phone. Blaze was calling. Emotion surged through her. Life had changed so much in the last few days. She knew healing was happening in her heart, but it was all so new. 'Hello, Blaze.'

'You're sounding chirpy this morning.'

She laughed. 'That's good, I guess. How are you?'

There was silence and Starre knew he was taken aback by the question. She never asked how he was. She just answered his questions in a sullen tone and wished he would finish the call.

'I'm well, I guess,' he said, as though he'd never even thought about it. 'How about you?'

'Chirpy.'

He laughed a deep, rumbling laugh and she loved the sound. She knew she'd caused her brother pain and concern at her coldness toward him and she wished she'd made more effort to be pleasant.

When he stopped laughing he sounded hesitant. 'Starre, I have a question for you. Feel free to tell me I'm out of line asking you, but I thought you'd be the best one …'

'Go ahead.'

'Sky wants a rescue horse. Prince offered her one of his own specially bred and trained horses, but I don't think she's ever forgiven him for abandoning her. There are real issues there. She insists she needs to give a home to one who needs her love and care.'

Starre heard his deep sigh on the other end of the phone. 'I just don't know what to do; what to think. You work with rescue animals. Are they good therapy for hurting teenagers? Would she be able to give it the care it needs?'

Starre was stunned. Sky was hurting? She felt abandoned? But she always looked so happy in the photos she was sent. She was doing so well in everything she put her hand to.

Like me. I appear so in control but deep down the pain of Chase's rejection stole my life and joy.

The irony of it was that she did have a suitable rescue horse. Prince's own horse—Regal Zion. Also abandoned by Prince, badly wanted by her but legally belonging to Chase. She took a deep breath. 'Let me think about it.'

Blaze let out another sigh. 'Thanks. I appreciate it.'

She shoved her phone back in her pocket, her thoughts racing. She desperately wanted to see Chase again. And she had an excuse. She had forgotten to get him to sign the form she had filled out about Regal Zion. It was as good an excuse as any.

Starre could hear Chase's voice before she even reached his room. He was telling someone a story.

'And so Courte stood there with the tap in her hand, just staring at me while water gushed out all over the room. She was completely soaked.'

'And not happy, I imagine.' The other voice was female and Starre hesitated. It seemed Chase was never in need of female company.

'No, not happy at all.' His voice was wistful and Starre thought about leaving but the woman was now at the door and saw her.

She looked back at Chase. 'Looks like you've got another official visitor.'

Chase looked up and saw her standing there, clipboard under

her arm. He smiled. 'No, not a visitor. A friend.'

The woman's brows rose. 'I'm not a friend?'

Chase grinned. 'I'd better be careful how I answer that or you might torture me unnecessarily.' He glanced to Starre. 'This is Jo, my OT.'

Jo smiled warmly. 'And clearly not a friend. Not in the sense you are, anyway.'

Chase shook his head. 'Come on Jo, don't be like that. It's just I've known Starre since we were kids.'

Jo's eyes widened. 'And you picked Courtney?'

Warmth filled Starre's cheeks and she dared not look at Chase. Why did people presume everyone wanted her just because she was physically attractive? It wasn't how it worked. Any decent male went further than that and looked at the heart. Being outwardly beautiful could prove a real barrier to finding someone who truly loved her for who she was.

Jo seemed to sense she had overstepped a boundary and with a nod of her head called back to Chase. 'I'll be back tomorrow. And think about what I said, okay?'

Starre dared to look back at him. His scars were less pronounced today, but it was clear they would be there for life.

He sat in a chair by the window, his eyes warm as he studied her. 'Come into my parlour.'

Starre grinned. 'Sounds ominous.'

'Believe me, it is.' His grey eyes were twinkling as he used his good leg to push a chair toward her. He glanced away. 'Sorry about Jo. She hasn't learned to filter what she says, but she's good at what she does.'

'What exactly does she do?'

'She's my occupational therapist. We've been talking about my future.'

Starre studied him. He looked sad. 'And?'

'I may not be able to continue in my job. I knew it was a

possibility.' He looked down at his damaged leg. 'I have femoral nerve dysfunction. The bullet did a bit of damage as it went through. I may always need a brace to support my knee. I'll never be as steady on my leg again.'

Starre felt his sadness down to the pit of her stomach. Chase had always been so active and fit. As a child she remembered him always moving, always running.

'I guess Courtney will be happy if you're not putting yourself in danger anymore.'

He didn't answer, but looked out the window, avoiding her gaze. Clearly she'd overstepped a boundary too. 'Sorry.'

He looked back to her, then. 'It's fine. Courtney's having a bit of trouble adjusting to some of the changes, that's all.'

Starre shook her head. 'If she can't see past your scars to what's inside you, then she's—'

'It's not just the scars. There's a lot more going on.'

She stopped, feeling guilty. He shouldn't have to defend his own partner.

'There's a possibility I can't have children now.' He said the words in a low, tired voice. 'When I was shot ... well, the damage went further than my leg. Courtney's always wanted a baby of her own.'

Starre looked away. What should she say? What *could* she say? It didn't seem fair. 'I'm so sorry, Chase.'

He didn't answer and she forced herself to look at him. He was looking out the window again, as though he wished he could be out there, running again. She cleared her throat. 'I forgot to get you to sign this form the other day.'

His eyes shot back to her and rested on the folder. He reached for it, then took a pen from his top pocket. 'So where's it up to?'

'No criminal charges will be laid. And when you're ready for Regal Zion you can have him back.' She paused and he studied her. He seemed to know she had more to say. She drew in a deep sigh. 'But can I visit him?'

Chase's smile came wide and full. 'Of course. As long as you visit me at the same time.'

She grinned. 'I think that's a given.'

He scribbled his name beside the cross at the end of the form and handed the folder back to her. 'What would have happened to him if I wasn't allowed to have him back?'

'I would have taken him.'

He nodded as though he'd known the answer already.

'Or I might have given him to Sky.' She didn't know why she admitted it to him. She hadn't even admitted it to herself yet.

'Sky Clements?'

She nodded, then stood and paced the room, wondering how much to tell him. He seemed to read her thoughts as he patted the chair again. 'Talk to me, Starre. I don't have much to do these days. I have plenty of time to listen.'

Slowly, her gaze holding his, she came and sat back down. She bit her nail and he leaned forward, pulling her finger from her mouth.

'So ...?'

'Blaze called me. Sky wants a rescue horse to love. Prince offered to give her one of his home bred, trained ones but she refused to take one from him. Blaze indicated she's never got over the fact that he abandoned her.'

Chase frowned. 'I can understand that.'

Starre shook her head. 'But she's so loved. Bonnie and Blaze dote on her. She has everything she could ever want. She's talented, beautiful, spoiled even.'

'But she's looking for love in the wrong place. A bit like you.'

Starre's eyes widened as indignation filled her. 'What's that supposed to mean?'

'You're still single, aren't you?' It was a statement, not a question. 'How many hearts have you broken? How many men have you rejected?'

He was getting way too personal. How dare he? She should just walk right out of there, with her completed form, this time, and never come back. But something in his grey eyes held her there.

He sighed. 'Starre, you're beautiful but I can tell you're different from the little girl I knew and loved. You're guarded. Sad. There's this great big barrier you've put up. You've lost your sparkle.'

When she didn't speak, he reached and pushed a wisp of dark hair from her face, tucking it behind her ear. It felt too close and personal, but she sat frozen in place, unable to make herself move. He sighed. 'You should never have loved me the way you did.'

'But there's no one else like you!' Her words burst out before she could stop them.

His mouth turned up in one corner. 'Have you even looked?'

'Of course not.'

There was a twinkle in his eyes now but he didn't smile. 'Starre, maybe your brother was right about his God. Blaze tried to tell me I would never find what I was searching for until I turned to God. I think Sky is looking for love in Prince instead of accepting what she has in Blaze. I think maybe you were searching for love in me instead of in God.'

Starre couldn't believe what she was hearing. That Chase would even talk about God was beyond her understanding. Part of the reason they had left the circus was Marcos' insistence that God and circus people didn't mix. When Blaze became a Christian it caused an uproar. Blaze had no longer been willing to follow everything Marcos expected and demanded, and Marcos didn't leave any room for a king other than himself in the little circus kingdom he had created.

Chase shuffled his feet and rubbed his knee as though it were hurting. 'I've spoken to a chaplain a few times in here. What he has to say actually makes a lot of sense.'

Starre sighed. 'I'm the only one in my family who hasn't embraced this whole Christianity thing,' she admitted. 'But Sky has, and apparently she's not happy like the others. Blaze said she still has issues.'

Chase nodded. 'Maybe she hasn't understood it. Not properly.'

Starre saw the sincerity in his eyes and knew that he still loved Sky. So why did the thought of the girl annoy her? Why could she feel no real warmth or compassion? She had become hard-hearted without even being aware. She didn't like who she'd become.

CHAPTER NINE

The campsite was a hive of activity as parents arrived with their children. Sky remembered how left out she had felt last year when everybody else was talking about their mother and father and she only had an uncle and aunty to care for her. But she refused to let herself feel that way any longer.

'I've lived this long without you, Dad,' she whispered fiercely, 'and I don't want you interfering and hurting me again now that I've learned to survive without your love. I'll help Joanna and Alexa to cope without their parents too!'

She lifted her chin, swung her hair and headed into the main hall.

It was emptier than usual, and heaviness weighed on her heart. Charles and Marion had confided in her their fears for the camp centre. Government regulations were making it harder to keep it up to standard. It required a lot of time and money; things Charles and Marion didn't really have. Camps were getting smaller as young adults spent more time in the world of technology.

Camp Oaken needed something more to draw people in. That's why the managers had been looking at bringing in horses. Horse riding seemed to attract campers.

'Sky! I was hoping and hoping you'd be back this year!' a voice cried, and Sky turned to Kathina Davies with a cry of delight.

'Of course I'm back,' Sky laughed, as she gave the large girl a hug. 'How could I miss camp?'

'How could anyone miss camp?' Kathina said. She gave Sky another impulsive hug. 'God used you to change my life. I want you to know that.' There were tears in the girl's eyes as she stepped back. 'You accepted me and loved me for who I am. It gave me a glimpse of God's love. Thank you.'

Sky swallowed hard, overwhelmed. What could she say? God had used her to touch someone's life for eternity; to introduce them to God. It was a privilege she couldn't comprehend.

'Sky, you're here at last!' Sky and Kathina both turned as Adelle ran and threw her arms around her. 'Guess what? I'm in your study group!'

Sky laughed with delight at her best friend from school. Adelle hadn't missed a camp yet. 'Dellie, where's Marion? I have to go and give her a big, sloppy kiss. I can't believe we're sharing study groups again! She must have forgiven us …'

'Forgiven you for what?' a deep voice interrupted, and Sky and Adelle turned at once to see Dallas Bourke standing behind them.

'Nothing,' Adelle said immediately, but Sky was laughing as she looked up at the young man who had tried so hard to get her attention the year before.

'Dellie tried to play a trick on—' Sky began.

Adelle cut her off. 'If I remember correctly it was your idea, Sky Clements.'

'Well, what happened?' Dallas demanded while the two girls argued back and forth.

Finally, Sky looked at him with a dazzling smile. 'Sorry, Dallas. We can't let you in on the details until we've established whose fault it really was.'

'But you two will never sort that out.'

Adelle and Sky shrugged at the same time. 'Sorry,' they said in unison and Dallas walked off. Sky could still hear him chuckling as he walked out the door.

She glanced around the room, wondering which of the girls were Joanna and Alexa. Her gaze stopped. A young man with an oval face, a cleft chin and neat, wavy blond hair stood across the hall. Her heart did a funny leap in her chest. She didn't think she knew him. Intrigued, she leaned in close to Adelle. 'Who's that?'

'That's Paul Seton. A bit of a dream, isn't he?'

Sky studied him. His chiselled features were serene and he turned slightly. His eyes were a warm brown. She swallowed. What had made her heart respond this way? There was something about him she couldn't put her finger on. Like a knowing; a recognition there was something significant about him.

God, is this what it means when people talk about love at first sight? Please settle my heart. Help me think clearly.

Instead of settling, her heart began to pound. Maybe she had just set eyes on the man she was going to marry. Why else would her usually careful heart respond in such a way? She'd never had this reaction to anyone before.

I'm going to get to know him. She watched as he moved to speak with Kathina. He obviously knew the rather chubby girl and laughed at something she said. The warm way he looked at her said she was special to him.

Sky smiled. It was unusual for such a good-looking guy to take time for Kathina. He must be humble as well. She should have no trouble capturing his attention, but hopefully he was someone who would look deeper and love her character, not just her appearance.

A group had begun to surround Paul and Kathina. Sky moved to join them. They made way for her and she gave a playful smile.

'Good to see you all again.' She looked at the familiar faces, 'I hope you've matured since last year.'

'You think we need to mature?' one of them demanded.

But she had turned her attention to Paul. 'I'm Sky.' She hoped her smile came across as more confident than she felt. Why was she so nervous? No other guy affected her this way. 'I hear you're Paul Seton.'

'That's right.' He just looked at her, not even offering a smile in return. Those warm brown eyes were not quite as warm as they had been when she'd seen him speaking to Kathina.

Respond, Sky. Say something sensible. 'Any relation to Hamish Seton the politician?'

'Not that I know of.'

His answers were off-handed, but Sky persisted. Her heart was still beating crazily and she tried to be as natural as possible. She tilted her head to the side. 'Seton isn't a common name. I've got a step-brother somewhere called Seton. Bit strange for a first name if you ask me.'

'Seton is known to be a first name.' Paul frowned. He didn't seem impressed by her attempt to be friendly.

'Maybe. It's not common, though.' She forced another smile. 'His twin's name is Blythe. Now that's definitely a surname. Maybe her parents liked Anne of Green Gables or something.'

Paul continued to study her, looking unamused. 'Blythe is also known to be a first name. It means "joyous".'

Sky grinned, trying not to be put off by his first reaction to her. Maybe his heart was beating as crazily as hers and he was trying to hide it. Or maybe it was just that he didn't know her yet. That was okay. She didn't want him to like her for her appearance. She wanted him to get to know her a whole lot better than that. She wanted him to love her for who she was deep down inside.

Love? The word had slipped into her subconscious before she could stop it. She smiled. She might as well admit it. Having Paul Seton love her would be a dream come true. Despite being cautious with her relationships, she was a romantic at heart, looking forward to the day she would meet the man she would marry. Meeting him would settle that ache somewhere deep inside. And whatever she was feeling toward Paul right now was confusing but special.

Sky was about to speak again when Marion, the camp manager came to her side. 'So you've met Paul,' she said, whilst giving Sky a delighted hug.

'Yeah, kind of.' Sky glanced at him, hoping he would notice Marion's friendly manner and realise how lovable she really was.

'Good. He's co-leading your study group.'

Sky smiled. 'Great. We'll get to know each other more!'

Paul gave her a look she couldn't define, then turned back to his friends, leaving her puzzled.

He's just nervous or shy, she told herself, then shrugged. If anyone knew how to bring a person out of their shell, she did.

Chapter Ten

'What's this?' Kathina demanded as she gazed around the camp cabin. The spaces on the walls were now filled with a wall hanging and the posters of horses Sky had added at the last minute. She gazed from one picture to the next, wondering at how the bright pictures transformed the stark little room.

'This is our home for a week and we can't have it looking plain.' She laughed, then pulled something else from her suitcase.

'What's that?' Kathina fingered the material Sky handed her.

'Curtains.'

'What?'

'I got them from my room. They'll need adjusting, though.'

Kathina's eyes widened. 'You can't just cut up the curtains from your bedroom.'

Sky grinned. 'Yes I can. Bonnie usually lets me get new ones every year. I like change. Now remember, Kathina, you said you like to sew?'

'When?' The girl's eyes showed her amusement.

'Last year. In the getting-to-know-you game where we had to share what we like to do in our spare time. We want to make this cabin ours!'

'You remember that?'

'Of course.'

Kathina smiled, then shook her head as she glanced at the

horse pictures again. 'Is this really our cabin or is it yours?''

'Ours, of course.' Sky gave a cheeky grin. 'I bring the posters, you make the curtains and Dellie can help set up. I know she's not in our cabin, but I reckon she'll spend most of her time with us anyway. We're all taking part in it.'

'What about the other girls?' Kathina frowned.

Sky fell silent for a moment. 'I don't even know them,' she finally admitted, 'but as soon as I discover their gifts, they're going to be a part of all this too.'

'What if one of them has a phobia of horses?'

She hesitated, then saw that Kathina was teasing. 'Then her part in all this can be to take the posters down again.'

'What if she can't even bear to look at the pictures? My sister got bitten by a wombat when she was little, and she shudders every time she even sees a picture of one.'

'Kathina!' Sky chastised with a laugh. 'Must you make reality out of your crazy imaginings? There can't be a girl on the face of this earth who's afraid of horses!'

The girl let out a snort. 'My imaginings? Here's a girl who thinks everybody in the world loves horses just because she does, and she thinks that I'm the one with the wild imagination!'

Sky just shook her head and began making her bed. She glanced up to see Kathina watching her, biting her lip. 'What?'

She shook her head. 'I just thank God for you. I don't think you realise how beautiful you are, inside and out.'

Sky was moved. Kathina and Adelle were true friends who loved her for who she was. They shared their love of God and it made them closer than any other friend could be. 'Thank you,' she whispered, overwhelmed.

Kathina looked down at the material again. 'I didn't bring scissors or thread or anything.'

Sky gave her a dazzling smile. 'Have you forgotten what I'm like already?' She reached into her suitcase and pulled out a needle, thread and scissors. Kathina's mouth dropped open.

'I even brought hanging rails.' Sky pulled the dismantled rail from her bag.

Kathina let out a hoot of laughter. 'There truly isn't anyone else in the world like you, Sky Clements!'

'I think we can all be grateful for that.'

Two more faces appeared at the door and Sky gave them a wide smile of welcome. 'How are you going?' she said. 'You must be Joanna and Alex.'

Neither girl responded. Sky's heart went out to them. 'Which beds would you like? I've claimed this one, but I'm quite willing to give it up if you want it.'

'What?' Kathina demanded, looking up from where she was already stitching curtains together. 'You wouldn't give it up for me.'

'Of course I would have!' Sky grinned. 'You just never asked me.' She turned back to the girls.

'This is Kathina. Kathina, this is Joanna and Alex.'

'Alexa,' the taller, more sullen of the girls corrected, and Sky managed not to be hurt by the cold tone of her voice.

'Alexa,' she repeated cheerfully not letting her smile dim.

Both girls selected a bed, then began unpacking. Alexa's expression was still hard, but Sky saw the way Joanna was looking around with interest, her eyes brightening as she saw the pictures of horses. It had been the right thing to bring them, no matter how immature some people might think it was.

'Who's this?' Sky asked as a photo fell from Joanna's Bible and fluttered onto the floor.

'That's my mum.'

Sky stared in awe at the picture. 'She's beautiful!'

'Yes,' she agreed quietly. 'She was.'

'Was?' Sky knew from Marion's report the beautiful woman had been murdered, but wanted to give Joanna a chance to talk about it.

Before she could, Alexa looked up, an expression of disgust across her face. 'Don't pretend not to know about us, Sky. I don't know what your game is, but I happen to know that wherever we go, people are warned about us first.'

Sky was shocked speechless, but managed to gather herself together when she saw Joanna's distressed look. *Help me know what to say, God. Help me show your love to these girls.* She should just be open and honest. 'You're right. I do know the basics about you, but I think you'd agree that knowing the basic facts doesn't really let me know who you are. I want to hear things from your own mouths. I don't want to just go on the "warnings", as you call them.'

Alexa's face softened as she turned back to make her bed. Sky noted the way she fastidiously tucked in each corner, then set her pillows straight. She determined then to keep her own things tidy for the sake of pleasing the unhappy girl.

With that thought, she turned back to Joanna to find she had carefully placed the photo back in her Bible and begun making her bed. The opportunity had passed, but Sky prayed for another chance to speak with her about her mother.

Chapter Eleven

'I hear the horse cabin is all set up.' Dallas gave Sky a wry smile as she wandered into the conference hall, Adelle and Kathina by her side. Joanna and Alexa followed a little way behind, their heads down.

'Horse cabin?' Sky put her hands on her hips. 'Who are you calling a horse?'

Dallas merely smiled at her playful indignation 'I said "horse cabin", not *horse's* cabin.'

'Perhaps you did but we all know horse is plural.'

Dallas frowned doubtfully. 'It is?'

Sky cast him a final glance. 'Gotcha.' She let out a merry laugh before moving to greet the campers filling the hall. She knew Dallas stared after her and that many of the campers who had overheard were chuckling. Chairs scraped as everyone found a seat.

'First, I'll introduce you to your leaders,' Marion told the campers as they settled into quietness. Sky glanced around, noting those who were there for the first time, most looking a little lost. She would make an effort to get to know them. When Sky Clements was in the camping scene, she was in her element.

'We have Dallas Bourke who was here last year. Stand up, Dallas.'

Dallas did so and a cry went up. 'Dally! Dally! Dally!'

Dallas merely grinned before plonking himself back into his seat.

'We also have Jake Timms … of course.'

Jake! Sky hadn't seen him come into the room and wished she could go and hug him straight away. Instead, she beamed at him while he stood in his mature, steady way and smiled at the campers. Only a few campers chanted his name before becoming embarrassed and falling quiet.

'Good to be here,' he told the group. He then stretched. 'I've come such a long way just to see you all.'

'Yeah, what's it like two metres from your house?' someone called out amidst chuckles.

Jake grinned. 'Hey, come on, it has to be at least ten metres! Anyway, I look forward to getting to know you all.'

Marion waited until the chatter died down. 'And we have Paul Seton. Paul's family are considering joining our staff and his parents will be here later in the week. Paul will also help lead our singing.'

Sky listened in interest, her heart beating faster. If he were to move here she would see a lot more of him. Was his family the answer to her prayers for the camp centre? Is that why she felt this way about him? Was that was God was telling her? No, she was sure it was more than that.

'We also have Sky again,' Marion announced as Sky stood and smiled around at everyone. She stopped at Paul at the end of the row. Finally his eyes met hers, but they almost imperceptibly narrowed. What was his problem? She wasn't sure but neither was she worried. She had never met anyone who didn't like her. Soon he'd feel the same way about her as she did about him.

'And we have Tabitha Morgan and Louise Turnbull,' Marion continued. 'Assisting our leaders are Kathina, Adelle …'

As the campers were divided into their Bible study groups, Sky tried to keep her focus away from her co-leader and on the campers. It wouldn't do to be distracted by the mysteriously confident Paul Seton.

'I thought we could begin by—' she began as the group settled.

To her surprise, Paul interrupted in his quiet, deep voice. 'Let's introduce ourselves,' he said, as though Sky were not even there, 'beginning with you.'

He turned to the boy sitting to his right. He shuffled uncomfortably, then looked up at Paul. 'You already know who I am.'

'I do,' Paul agreed with a slow smile, 'but the rest of them don't.'

The boy gave an embarrassed grin, then managed to glance at a few of the people in the group. 'I'm Harrison Davies.'

'Kathina's brother?' Sky had recovered from her surprise at Paul's interruption and didn't bother to hide her delight at meeting someone connected to Kathina.

Harrison nodded slightly and looked back down at his shoes, but he sat a little taller.

'Tell us a bit about yourself,' Paul urged, before casting Sky a disapproving look. Sky met his gaze without flinching, though his reaction was confusing.

'I'm thirteen and I'm Kathina's brother,' was all he could come up with.

Sky, the natural conversation maker, couldn't help taking over once again. 'So where do you live? What are your interests?'

She noticed the way Paul fell silent and sat back as she skilfully brought each member of the group out of their shyness and into open, friendly discussion. If Paul had been younger she would think he was sulking.

'And you're Paul,' she finished, turning to him.

'I'm Paul.'

'Anything else?' Her tone was playful. 'Do you have brothers or sisters?'

'Yeah.'

Sky chuckled at his reluctance to share. He must be shy. She'd give him his space. She turned to Harrison Davies. 'Well, Davo, maybe you can tell us a bit about Paul since you know him.'

'Davo? He already told us his name is Harrison.'

Sky started at the snap in Paul's tone. No, definitely not shy. Something else was going on here. She forced a grin. 'I know. But we used to call Kathina Davo. Now she's grown out of it, we can pass the name along to Harrison.'

Harrison grinned in delight at the privilege of taking on his sister's old nickname. 'Paul's got lots of horses and he rides real good,' he said quickly, almost running his words together in his haste to oblige Sky's request.

'Thanks, Davo.' Sky glanced at Paul. He loved horses. He was more like her than she realised. Despite his lack of warmth, the way she had seen him relate to Kathina encouraged her. She would break down the barriers he had put up. He was worth the effort, despite the way he was now looking at her through guarded eyes.

***

Sky noticed every time Paul Seton was in a room. He stood tall and poised, silently watching everything going on around him. He noticed when any camper stood alone and made his way toward them, sitting with them in quiet conversation.

He spent a lot of time with Kathina Davies, working with her as a team, smiling almost every time she spoke and appearing more at home with her than any of the other campers. On many occasions Sky saw him put an arm around her shoulder. There was definitely some kind of connection between them. But was it romantic or just a deep friendship?

Her admiration for Paul increased when the group began their time of singing. Paul led in his quiet, confident manner and his deep, mellow voice filled the room, leaving goose bumps on her skin. Not only was he appealing in his appearance and manner, his voice was pure music, whether singing or speaking.

She had known from the moment she first saw him that he was special and that conviction grew with everything she heard him say and all she saw him do.

All that first day, Sky felt as though she were walking in a dream. And as the night closed in, it seemed even harder to live in reality and focus on those she was responsible for.

'Grow up and get over your infatuation,' she told herself as her heart once more let her know Paul was approaching. Her cabin sat with her around the campfire, waiting for the others to arrive. Jake Timms was there with his group, early as usual.

'How are you all going?' Sky gave a cheerful wave. Paul barely gave a nod of recognition, while his group responded heartily, assuring Sky they were having a wonderful time.

To Sky's surprise, the seemingly shy Paul led that time around the campfire with an easy confidence. He spoke of God's love for his children so much like a father's love.

Paul looked around the group, his brown eyes reflecting the flickering of the campfire. 'The difference is, our human fathers let us down, but our Heavenly Father never will. He always keeps his promises.'

Sky shuffled uncomfortably. She was very much aware of the theme for this camp was the Father's love and hoped it didn't dig deeper into her heart than she wanted to go.

Paul lifted a guitar from a case on the ground and put the strap over his shoulder. 'I'm going to sing you a song my sister wrote.' He began gently strumming the guitar and the group fell silent. All that could be heard was the crackling of the campfire and the sound of Paul's fingers across the strings of his guitar. Sky gazed at him, enjoying the way the flames lit up his now expressive face.

'It's called "Clinging to the Promise",' he said, then began to sing.

Clinging to the rainbow,

I know your promise stands,
your sky is lit by sunset
held in loving hands.

At times it disappears yet
I know my eyes can't see
all life's eternal moments
you have planned for me.

Clinging to your promise
I know you rose on high
and in the morning I will
behold the dawn lit sky.

Yes, clinging to the rainbow
although it may be night,
I know your promise stands
in everlasting light.

Clinging to the promise,
Your love has given me,
That I will live forever,
I'm yours eternally.

Sky's heart began its crazy beating again, touched by the words and moved by the music.

Paul gazed around at the silent group. 'We can cling to our Heavenly Father's promises, even when we don't understand his plan. In fact, especially when we don't understand his plan. We can trust him.

Sky swiped at her eyes, overwhelmed. She needed time to think and pray.

'You okay?' Kathina's concerned voice came quietly in her ear.

She drew in a deep breath. 'I will be.'

Kathina gave her a quick hug. 'You go and take some time

out. I'll prepare our cabin for bed.'

Sky studied her. She couldn't do that. It wouldn't be fair. But Kathina smiled. 'Let me do this for you, Sky. You've been such a blessing to me.'

God, if I refuse it will just be my stubborn pride not allowing Kathina to help. Help me be gracious.

Taking a deep breath, she nodded. 'Thanks, Kathina. I appreciate it.'

She headed off in the opposite direction of the cabins, looking up into the night sky. Stars twinkled overhead. They were much easier to see out here away from the city. God felt closer, somehow.

God, I clung to my father's promise and got burned. Bitterness built up inside her, stronger than she'd expected. *I should have known, though. Everything about his past life shows he's not dependable.*

'What are you doing out here?' a deep voice asked and Sky jumped, turning to see Paul.

'Walking. Thinking.'

'Aren't you supposed to be getting your cabin ready for bed?'

Sky chuckled. 'As are you.'

'They're in bed already.' His tone sounded accusing.

'I expect mine are too. Kathina is helping out.' She hesitated. 'Thank you for your leading and singing tonight. I appreciated it.'

Paul frowned and she wondered if it was because he doubted Kathina's ability to handle the cabin or if he didn't think she was genuine in her thanks. He gave a dismissive wave of his hand and disappeared into the night.

As she wandered the camp centre, Sky felt the heaviness in her heart deepen. She loved this place. She would be devastated if it had to close.

'Please, Lord, bring more people here to hear about you,' she prayed. 'And please provide Charles and Marion with the workers and money they need to keep it all going. Thank you for the blessing this camp has been in my life.'

Chapter Twelve

Sky didn't sleep well. She'd awoken to hear Joanna muttering in her sleep. She couldn't distinguish the words, but could tell they were disturbed.

She allowed thoughts of Paul and the troubled girls in her room to run around her head. If she didn't think about them, thoughts of her own mother's death and her father's broken promise would squeeze around her heart.

Finally, around six o'clock in the morning she decided it was no longer worth sleeping. She headed off for a shower.

'So you're planning to win points in your dorm by being creative rather than neat, are you?' an amused voice called as she came back from the showers. She looked up to where Jake sat by the old campfire, Bible in his lap. Jake was always so dedicated, whatever he did, and Sky couldn't help feeling guilty that she hadn't made time to spend alone with God each morning.

She stopped and gave him a pointed look. 'It's much more fun to be creative.'

He chuckled, running a hand through his ginger hair. 'It's much easier to be organised and dignified. I don't like chaos.'

'Dignified?' Sky headed toward him, drying her wet hair with a towel as she walked. 'You don't think chaos is dignified? What about organised chaos? Surely you've heard of that?'

Jake's lips twitched. 'Heard of it, but never seen it happen in real life. And you're looking a bit wild and out of control this morning.'

He was looking up at her dark hair which she knew was in a tangled mess now that she'd rubbed it dry. She must look a sight. She couldn't help smiling at him. 'It's so good to see you again, Jake.'

He smiled back, his eyes twinkling at her. 'You too. I look forward to catching up some more.'

She left him to go and find her brush and hair dryer. Jake had an inner strength and depth of character she admired. The first time she'd met him he'd been a nervous wreck. Adelle had pointed out the truth—he was attracted to her and it threw him. Sky had quickly let him know she wasn't interested in anything other than friendship and his romantic attraction had either died or their developing friendship had overcome it. They now shared a special connection she cherished.

Determined not to be distracted by Paul again, Sky deliberately sat with Alexa and Joanna at breakfast. Adelle sat opposite, playing the usual immature tricks of putting salt in the sugar container and jam inside the butter wrappers. Sky shook her head at her friend, reminding her they were leaders and had to control themselves to some extent. Joanna and Alexa sat stony faced, and Sky prayed for a way to break through to them.

'You don't have to sit with us, you know,' Alexa said coldly, catching Sky's gaze as breakfast finished.

'I know, but I want to.'

'Well we don't want you to. Have you ever thought of that or are you too used to everyone loving you and feeling honoured if you even look at them?'

Stung by her words, Sky managed to chuckle, but for once had no response. She felt rather than saw the way Adelle stiffened as though about to retaliate, but managed to give her friend a look to silence her. She knew Adelle wasn't fooled by her smile of reassurance but she let the matter go.

Adelle walked by Sky's side as they made their way to the

morning session. 'So are we going to sit with the horror sisters again?'

'Dellie!'

Adelle shrugged. 'Well, they are.'

Sky turned and what she saw chilled her to the bone. Joanna stood not far away and was looking at Adelle, obviously having heard the comment. Her eyes were filled with a cold hate, the closest to evil that she'd ever seen. And yet, just as quickly the look disappeared.

Joanna caught her eye and gave her a small wave and a pleasant smile, leaving her even more confused. Had she been imagining the look in the girl's eyes? She didn't think so; in that split second it had been all too clear.

Go carefully, a voice in her heart warned, and Sky turned away. She grabbed Adelle by the hand and pulled her to where Paul Seton sat in the row of chairs. 'We'll sit here.'

Adelle gave her a look. 'With someone else who doesn't want your company?'

Hurt by her comment, Sky looked away but continued her progress to the seat beside Paul. She was sure he just needed to get to know her a bit more. He had no reason to dislike her the way Alexa and Joanna did.

'You can share with me,' she offered as she moved closer to him, her Bible open at the place Jake had directed the group.

Paul gave a polite shake of his head and moved to help the boy on his other side find the right page. It was clear he wasn't someone she could impress with her friendly nature and bubbly personality. His focus seemed to be only those who needed pity. The unattractive, emotionally needy ones.

She had seen him with his arm casually slung around Kathina's shoulder again that morning. He seemed comfortable with the large, pimple faced girl, so what was his problem with her? *It will just take time. Once he gets to know me ...*

'You're pretty close to Paul Seton,' Sky ventured when Kathina sought her out at morning tea time.

Kathina glanced to where Paul stood across the other side of the room chatting with Harrison. 'Yeah, we go to the same school. When I became a Christian and started going to the Christian group at school he was really supportive. I always say you were the one who made me see my need of Christ, and he's the one who helped me grow in Christ.'

'So you have feelings for him?'

Kathina baulked at the question, her face becoming slightly pink. 'Well,' she began slowly as though unsure of her own answer, 'I think he's the best friend I've ever had. But I'm not the sort of girl a guy has romantic feelings for, and if I started to have feelings like that for him, it might ruin the best friendship I've ever had.'

'So he doesn't think you have feelings for him?'

Kathina laughed openly at that. 'Of course not. I doubt he'd be as affectionate or comfortable with me if he thought I did!'

Sky smiled, satisfied. It was as she thought. The relationship between Paul and Kathina was purely one of friendship. And clearly Paul thought he could help her; that was his motivation.

Once more Sky found her eyes drawn to Paul. He was laughing at something Alexa had said to him. He gave her a friendly poke and she looked up at him with shy admiration.

'He's so good with his foster sisters,' Kathina said, and Sky's attention jerked back to her.

'Pardon?'

'His foster sisters. Joanna and Alexa live with him.'

That was news to Sky, but she was pleased with the new-found knowledge. Maybe Paul could give her some more insight into the two girls and their troubled pasts. Maybe he could help her get through to them.

A bell rang and everyone looked to Jake who stood on the stage. 'Come on, people, time to stop chatting. Take your seats.' He grinned at Adelle who had grabbed one and begun to carry it outside. 'I mean, for those who have trouble understanding simple English, come and sit down.'

Adelle rolled her eyes and came back.

Sky chuckled too, remembering the way she'd once thought Jake lacked a sense of humour. She now knew he was just careful and mature. He could have a good laugh and be funny when it was appropriate.

'Come on,' Sky encouraged those taking their time. 'You heard the Mayor of the South. Let's sit down.'

Jake stopped and raised an eyebrow, having heard her just as she intended. 'The Mayor of the South?'

She nodded. 'You're the man in charge over the south side of the camp, aren't you?'

He merely gave her an amused smile.

'He's so good!' Adelle said into her ear. 'I doubt he's ever been late for anything in his life.'

Sky grinned. 'There's always a first time.' A plan began to form. She needed to be mature and focus on the foster girls, but a bit of fun might be just what they needed to help break the ice. Besides, Jake was asking for it with his teasing her that morning about being 'wild and out of control'. If she didn't miss her guess, Jake and his cabin would be having an extended break time and would be late for lunch.

Sky disappeared as soon as the session finished. Girls weren't allowed in the boys' rooms, but she was sure she could get young Harrison to help her. He looked like a boy who would enjoy a bit of fun. 'Davo,' she called.

He turned to her with a shy smile as he waited for her to reach his side.

'Can you do me a favour?'

'Yeah, sure. Like what?'

'Turn a few clocks back fifteen minutes?'

Harrison's eyes widened as Sky told him her plan. Then he laughed, and she knew he would help.

Sky's next move was to find Kathina. Her eyes also lit up with amusement as she told her the next stage of her plan. Then she watched as Kathina made her way to Jake. The two spoke animatedly for a few moments before Jake undid the watch from his wrist and handed it to her.

Kathina came back to her with a huge grin. 'Too easy.'

'What did you tell him?'

'Just asked if I could borrow it for a minute for a game.' She looked sheepish. 'Well, it is kind of a game.'

Sky grinned as she began adjusting the time on the watch. 'Of course it is.' She handed the watch back to Kathina to return. 'Game on!'

***

Everyone was sitting at tables for lunch, except Jake's group. A rather noisy grace had been sung and Sky directed the first table in to get their lunch. She was about to direct the next table when the door opened and in came Jake's group. Before Jake's face could even register his surprise at seeing everyone sitting, some already eating, Sky came to him, forcing a frown on her face. 'You're late!'

Jake glanced at the clock on the wall and his face turned from confused to horrified.'But …' he glanced at his watch. 'Oh no, it's stopped!'

'You've got other clocks in your room. Are you trying to tell me no one in your group even looked at them? Or did they stop too?' Sky tried to keep a straight face but was struggling.

Jake met her eyes and understanding dawned. 'You … you schemer!' His mouth began to turn up in the corners. He put a hand up in an attempt to cover his amusement.

Sky laughed. 'Don't pretend to be angry, Jake. Your dimples give you away every time.'

'I don't have dimples,' he said through his fingers.

'Well, laugh lines or whatever they are.'

The group sitting around the closest table laughed, while Jake removed his hand to reveal a wide grin. 'Right, that's it!' he said with his hands on his hips. 'You're in big trouble, Sky Clements!'

'Big trouble? What kind of big trouble?'

'I'm taking you off my list of potential wives kind of trouble!'

The group whistled and banged on the table while Sky's eyes widened. 'You have a list?'

'Of course I do.'

Sky shook her head mischievously. 'Well, I must say I'm honoured I'm even on it.'

Jake waved a finger in her face and stepped back. 'Not anymore, you're not.'

Recklessly, Sky threw herself at him and held him like she would never let go. 'Oh, Jake, please have mercy. To be on there and then to be taken off is almost more than I can bear.'

Jake's expression showed his surprise at her theatrics before he began to laugh, pushing her back. 'Okay, okay, I won't scratch you off this time, but you'd better tread carefully from now on!'

Sky gave him a last squeeze. 'Thank you. You have no idea how much this means to me.'

Jake chuckled almost seriously. 'I think I do.'

His gaze met hers and she thought she caught a glimpse of hurt in those clear, open eyes. It threw her. She'd meant to have fun, not hurt someone. What worried her even more was the look Paul Seton was giving her. As though he thought she was flirting with Jake and didn't appreciate it. If she wanted to win Paul's heart she would need to be more careful.

Chapter Thirteen

Starre knew having Regal Zion at the rescue centre was distracting her from her work. Thinking about Chase was distracting her even more.

'How long until his owner gets out of rehab?'

Starre stopped stroking Regal Zion to look over at Jordan. He leaned against the fence. 'Not sure.'

'You should ask him. Get an idea how long you've got.'

She didn't bother to answer, wishing he'd go away. She'd made it clear she wasn't interested in him but he was constantly watching her, giving surreptitious glances when he thought she didn't see. It was irritating and made her uncomfortable.

He opened the gate and came in. She deliberately looked the other way, focusing her attention on Regal Zion.

'Is it just me or is it every male?'

Her eyes flew to his. 'What do you mean?'

'Have you got a problem with me personally? Have I offended you?'

She met his gaze and saw the vulnerability there. For the first time it bothered her the way she treated him. 'It's not you.'

'You do realise you're beautiful don't you? I don't look at you the way I do because I'm creepy or anything.' He gave a helpless shrug. 'You're beautiful.'

His blunt words shook her. He wasn't trying to flirt. He

was genuine.

'Not every guy is like the one who hurt you.'

She stiffened. 'Who says I've been hurt?'

He looked uncertain for a moment before he sighed. 'You act like the abused animals that are brought in here. The ones who are too scared to be touched. The ones that bite if you try to pat them or show you care. The ones terrified of the medical care we provide for their own good.'

Was he trying a new way of flirting; of getting around the barriers she had set in place? She narrowed her eyes. He didn't look like he was being clever and manipulative, but …

Her own cynical thoughts shook her. Couldn't she trust *anyone* anymore? Was she really like those caged animals, shying away from any kind of love?

'I'm not trying to crack onto you, Starre. I'd be stupid to after the way you reacted to my attention last time. I guess I just want you to be happy. To live and run free like Zara did when she was rehabilitated.'

His words struck a chord. Zara the greyhound had been brought in with a broken leg after an accident on the race track. Her owners had planned to put her down but a protester against greyhound racing had managed to save her. Zara paced her cage, snarling and snapping and refusing love and attention. Sky had to sedate her to give her the medical treatment she needed. However, by the end of her stay she had been transformed. It had taken much love and hard work, but seeing her run free, almost floating with abandon in the yard of her adopted family had left a lump in Starre's throat. Healing had come not just physically, but emotionally as well. Zara really did run free.

Will I ever be free? It was a question she knew she couldn't answer until she knew for sure what it was she needed to be freed from. Maybe she *was* like Sky. Not accepting love and healing because she had once looked in the wrong place and been hurt. A sudden need to see Sky welled up within her. Not just in pictures on her Facebook page and in emails, but in person.

***

'Even though he's not that nice to you, he looks at you a lot,' Adelle commented in Sky's ear as they watched Paul playing football with the boys from his cabin.

Sky said nothing, but she had noticed it too. Perhaps he was interested in getting to know her better but was too shy to make a move. She had never needed to do it before but maybe this time she needed to make the first move.

'Hey boys, can we play?'

Paul stopped, holding the football under his arm and looking back at her. 'Who's we?'

'My group. Kathina, Alexa and Joanna and me.'

He shrugged. 'Okay.'

Throwing a grin at Adelle, Sky ran to find the others. She soon had them rounded up, though Alexa insisted there was no way she was going to play with a bunch of rough boys.

'Come on, Lexi,' Paul coaxed, and Sky saw the way Alexa's face softened, though she still refused to play. Instead, she stood on the sidelines, watching them.

'Pass the ball, Joanna,' one of the boys called to her, then swore when she fumbled and dropped it. He came to retrieve it, but before he could, Joanna had grabbed him by the hair and thrown him to the ground. She was about to kick him when Paul stood in her way.

'That's enough, Joanna,' he said sternly, and once more Sky was chilled by the look in the girl's eyes. The hate there was frightening. Then, as fast as it came, it was gone.

'Sorry,' she muttered to the boy before the game continued.

Sky noticed Paul leave to get a drink from the tap and she followed discreetly, watching as he had a long drink, then ran a wet hand through his fair hair. He turned and started when he saw her.

'Do you think Joanna acts like that because of her mother's death?' Sky asked quietly.

Paul gave her a level look. 'Possibly.'

'Do you have any ideas how we can get through to her?'

His eyes narrowed, his expression turning hard. 'Model forgiveness for her. Make sure our own lives are right with God.'

Model forgiveness? What about her dad? It was easy for someone like Paul to say.

He headed back toward the group and Sky fell into step beside him. 'I really did appreciate your talk around the campfire the other night. It's got me thinking.'

'What about? Forgiving your father? Meeting him?'

Sky stopped as though she had been slapped. How did he know anything about her father? Someone must have told him … probably not the whole story, though. She would simply have to fill him in.

'I don't know what you've heard about my father but I'm not interested in getting to know him. He refused to admit I was even his until I was about two or three. Then he got this other woman pregnant—she's supposedly a Christian—and she converted my dad, or something. Funny way of converting, if you ask me. She must have a different set of beliefs from me!'

She saw Paul stiffen. For some reason he was angry. His brown eyes bored into hers. 'Are you ever going to forgive?'

Puzzled by the intensity of his question and the way he spat out the words, Sky swallowed hard. 'I've tried. I even wrote to tell him how much he hurt me and how I want to sort it all out but he didn't even answer.'

'Maybe you need to reconsider what you write,' Paul suggested. 'Stop seeing him as the one in the wrong.'

Sky stared at him. 'You talk as if you know me.'

'Sometimes you can know someone without having met them.'

What was he talking about? 'Why do you keep implying I'm

the one in the wrong? Dad's the one who needs to be forgiven.'

'Exactly! So forgive him!' Paul gave her a final pointed look before he jogged back onto the oval and rejoined the game.

Sky didn't know what to think of Paul Seton. He was so caring and compassionate to everyone, except her. At least her heart had stopped its crazy beating whenever he was nearby. She didn't feel like continuing the football game and so moved to a bench seat to sit down and watch.

As she bent to sit, Jake slid in beneath her and took her spot. She stopped and turned, grinning at the mischievous look on his face.

'Ooh, you're lucky!' She straightened and stepped back. 'I nearly sat on you!'

His mouth dropped open. 'Shock, horror!'

She titled her head, noting the smile lines around his eyes. 'You don't fool me. I saw the fear in your eyes.'

He shook his head, eyes twinkling at her. 'That wasn't fear. That was something completely different. I thought you were going to sit on my lap.'

For some reason Sky couldn't explain, a blush began to fill her cheeks.

'Sorry, I didn't mean to embarrass you.' Despite his apology, he couldn't hide the amusement behind his eyes. He patted the seat beside him. She sat.

'So how's it going with the foster sisters?' he asked.

She bit her lip. 'I'm a bit worried about them.'

'Me too. I've been praying for you as you deal with them.'

Warmth filled her heart at his concern and support. How could she express to Jake how grateful she was for him? He always good that way; so thoughtful and Godly. Trust him to remember to pray. 'Thanks, Jake.'

He looked steadily into her eyes, now confident rather than shy in her presence. 'Be careful, won't you?'

Before she could ask why, he stood abruptly and walked away. Sky watched him go, puzzling over his warning.

CHAPTER FOURTEEN

Sky held out her plate for the mashed potato. With a plop, Charles put it on her plate. Next came the peas, but she held her plate away. 'No thanks.'

'Come on, Sky,' Marion coaxed, 'Your mother said I had to look after you. That means making sure you have your veggies.'

Sky indicated to the mashed potato. 'I have my veggies.'

Behind her, Dallas took the opportunity for revenge. 'Remember, you're the expert on plurals, Sky. One is singular, two is plural. I don't see more than one vegetable on your plate.'

Sky gave a mock groan and held out her plate again. 'Okay, okay, put the peas on.'

Dallas grinned and put his free arm around her. 'That's my girl!'

Sky pretended to glare at him. 'I'm not your girl!'

Dallas grinned wider. 'What? Not even for today? Don't you have someone different every day? That's what I heard.'

Sky screwed up her nose at him before grinning. 'Ooh, that hurt!' Then she saw Paul behind Dallas. He had clearly heard and didn't look impressed. Impulsively, she stepped back and playfully put an arm around his shoulder. 'Paul is the only one for me.'

To her surprise, Paul pushed her arm away. 'I'm not yours to touch.' he said quietly but firmly into her ear.

Sky felt her face flame. 'I was just—'

'I know what you're about.' Paul's gaze met hers evenly.

'And I'm not free. For once, you can't have everything you want, Sky Clements.'

Confusion washed over her as she turned away. Paul seemed to have the wrong idea about her. Inside, the deep craving to be loved and understood burnt a hole in her heart. She needed Paul to accept her. To love her. She needed to let him know who she really was and how she felt about him, but whenever she was looking into that handsome face and melting brown eyes she couldn't think. She would have to write him a letter.

As Sky began, she felt guilty knowing Kathina had feelings for Paul too. At the same time, she was confident the girl would forgive her if she ended up in a relationship with Paul. Kathina was that type of girl—gentle, unassuming and sweet.

I know this letter may come as a surprise to you.

Sky looked at the words and chuckled. More than a surprise. A complete shock? She tapped the end of the pen on her chin and sighed. The words weren't coming easily.

'Lord, help me,' she prayed. 'You know how much this means to me.'

Talking to God renewed her confidence. She spoke openly to God about her feelings every day, apart from her feelings about her father, and she knew how to express her heart's deepest desires.

I have feelings for you. At first I held back, thinking you might have feelings for Kathina. She's a special friend of mine and I wouldn't want to hurt her, so if that's the case, please just tell me straight out. But if not, is it possible that you and I could get to know one another more? I know we haven't known each other for long, but from the first I admired your quiet strength and confidence. I love the way you care for those in need and I have great respect for you. And I love the way you sing. It gives me goose bumps just to listen to you singing to our God.

You seem to think I'm the type to fall for any guy I see. That's not true. I haven't felt this way about anyone else before. I don't really know what else to say, which is unusual for me. I don't think I've ever told a guy I love him before, but it's true. With love and hopefully mutual friendship, whichever way you decide,

Your co-leader,

Sky.

Sky re-read the letter a few times, then taking a deep breath, went in search of Paul. Camp probably wasn't the best place to develop a relationship, but she just had to know what Paul was thinking. It was way more distracting to dream and wonder than it would be to just know what was going on in his mind.

Paul was watching some younger boys on the flying fox. She approached him, the letter in her hand. His brown eyes met hers in a question.

'I have this for you.' Her heart was beating fast, her mouth dry. She'd had boyfriends before, so why was this such an issue?

Then it occurred to her. She was risking rejection; the thing she feared most in the world. Every other boyfriend had approached her first. This time she was the one putting her heart on the line.

'What is it?' Paul asked with a frown as he turned the envelope over.

Sky was about to answer when feet pounded across the ground toward them. Kathina was running, sucking in big breaths, her eyes wide. 'Alexa's in the kitchen with a knife. She said she's going to kill herself.'

Sky gasped. 'What?'

Paul put a hand on Kathina's arm. 'It's okay. She does it all the time. Let me deal with it.'

She did it all the time? Sky stood frozen, watching as Paul shoved her precious letter in his pocket and took off at a jog toward the kitchen.

Kathina doubled over, trying to catch her breath. It was clear she wasn't used to running. She coughed, then straightened, her eyes following the direction Paul had gone. 'He's amazing, Sky. He loves and cares for everyone.'

Sky frowned. 'I'm not sure that's the case with me.'

'I have to admit I don't know what he's got against you.'

'So you've noticed it? You think he's got something against me?' A sick feeling began to swirl around Sky's stomach. What had she just done, handing him that letter? Even Kathina had noticed the way he treated her.

She looked uncomfortable. 'Yeah. So you don't have any idea what it's about either?'

Sky frowned. 'No. I did wonder if he's trying to deny what he really feels. Jake used to be all uncomfortable and nervous around me before I made it clear I just wanted to be friends. Maybe this is Paul's way of dealing with unwanted feelings. But then again, he seems more mature than that.'

Kathina paled. 'You think he's in love with you?'

Sky bit her lip. 'I'm not sure. I mean, he's all compassionate to people like Alexa and Joanna …'

'And me?'

Sky fell silent.

'It's okay, Sky, I need to know. Do you think he's extra nice to me because he feels sorry for me?'

Sky looked at her friend in shock. She did. It was true. But why? Kathina was one of the most beautiful girls she knew. Maybe not in outward appearance, but her heart was deep and her personality loveable. Who did she, Sky Clements, think she was? Tears sprang to her eyes, and suddenly she gave her a fierce hug.

'Who do I think I am? I'm so sorry. I've done something terrible.'

Kathina looked lost, but her open expression assured Sky she was safe to confess what she had done. She listened quietly as Sky told her about the letter. 'I saw you as my competition and I don't want that. You're one of the sweetest friends I have.'

To her surprise, Kathina smiled. 'That's the biggest compliment anyone has ever paid me.'

Sky was puzzled. 'I'm sure many people have told you how sweet you are.'

'Not that,' Kathina said with a small laugh. 'Imagine someone like you seeing me as competition! A beautiful, talented, Godly girl who attracts the attention of every male who ever looks at her, actually sees me as competition.'

Sky stared at her and saw that she was serious. Unable to help herself, she began to laugh. Kathina did too and soon the girls were hugging and laughing through tears. She knew then, that whatever happened, she would never see Kathina Davies as less valuable. She was way more gracious and spiritual than she herself had ever been.

'Work in my heart to make me more like Kathina, Lord,' she found herself praying. 'That is, make me more like you!'

'Sky, there you are!' a deep, breathless voice called. Sky and Kathina withdrew from their embrace to see Jake standing there, concern furrowing his brow.

'Charles and Marion want you to go and speak with Alexa in the kitchen.'

Alexa! Sky had forgotten about her for a few minutes.

'Is everything okay?'

Jake nodded. 'I think so. Joanna and Marion are with her now.'

Sky breathed a sigh of relief, but Jake looked concerned.

'Be careful, Sky,' he said quietly, then left again. Why did he keep saying that? Sky couldn't work out why she needed to be careful of Alexa or Joanna. They were simply girls who needed to know God's love, and she intended to let them know about it.

Chapter Fifteen

Sky was cautious with the emotionally fragile Alexa. She was grateful for Kathina's support as the two tried to work out what had upset her so badly.

In the end it was Joanna who woodenly told them the story. 'One of the kids wouldn't wash up his cup and told Alexa to do it. Charles didn't realise it wasn't Alexa's and tried to make her. She grabbed a knife and said she'd kill herself.'

Sky couldn't believe it. Why would something so minor upset Alexa so much? Obviously there was a lot more going on in her troubled heart than she realised.

'It's okay,' Sky said, resisting the urge to call her Alex or Lexi.

Before she could continue, Alexa had cut her off. 'It's not okay, Sky. You and your grand ideas about Jesus and his love and giving and blah, blah, blah. You've never had a day of pain in your life!'

Sky's eyes met hers. 'My father abandoned me too.'

Alexa let out a harsh laugh. 'I wish my father abandoned me!'

'What do you mean?'

'My father always came home.' Alexa crossed her arms defensively across her chest. 'But I sure wished he wouldn't.'

Sky said nothing, but her eyes begged the girl to go on.

'He got angry so easily but I kept putting up with it, thinking it was my fault for provoking him. Then one day he didn't come home, and while I waited for him, I thought how much I really did want him, how if something happened to him, I would never forgive myself for so often wishing him dead.'

Alexa's hard, expressionless face softened for just a moment. 'So when he finally got home a few days later I told him I loved him, even though he was totally drunk. He looked so shocked, I realised that probably no one had ever told him that before.'

Alexa fell into silence.

'And what happened?' Sky pressed.

She shook her head, anguish filling her face. 'I don't want to talk about it.'

Sky watched as she stalked off. She wouldn't push it for now, but she would pray like she never had before. It was true, Sky had never known true pain, not like Alexa had.

A quiet voice spoke at her side. 'Don't listen to a word she says, Sky. She's a liar.'

Sky spun to face Joanna, unable to believe what the small girl had just said. She'd thought Joanna and Alexa were friends, the way they were constantly with each other, Joanna following Alexa around like a little puppy dog. Before Sky could question her, the girl headed off after her foster sister without another word.

'Well,' Sky breathed to Kathina. 'What do you make of that?'

She looked slightly pale. 'I have no idea. But like Jake says, maybe you should be careful.'

Sky had so much on her mind that she forgot about her letter to Paul. So it was a shock when that evening, as she stood in the kitchen washing up, he charged in.

'You're in love with me?' he demanded shaking the letter at her. 'How can you be? You don't even know me. Kathina and I have been friends for years. Do you really think you can compete with that just because you're attractive in a worldly way and popular because you tread everyone else down? I'm sorry Sky Clements, but it's Christ likeness that attracts me, and between you and Kathina … well, you're simply no match.'

Sky stared at him, speechless. She felt her cheeks becoming bright red, then let out a hollow chuckle. 'I'm sorry, Paul. I shouldn't have said it. It was the wrong time to tell you my feelings.'

'Wrong time? You can wait forever and it will still be the wrong time. You're shallow. You think you have it all together, you talk down your own father to complete strangers. You're a Pharisee! And unless you see that you're sick, you won't go to the doctor.'

'Well, I guess you've told me,' she said quietly, and continued drying the plate she was holding.

She was aware of the way Alexa, Joanna, Kathina and Marion were staring at Paul.

Suddenly Kathina found her voice. 'How could you, Paul? What's got into you? At home you're so thoughtful, compassionate and caring. You're someone totally different right now, and to tell you the truth, I really don't like you this way.'

Paul looked down for a moment, then his brown eyes met hers. 'Kathina, she's trying to make the moves on me because she thinks you're in love with me. She just likes the competition and she likes to believe she'll always win.'

Kathina shook her head at him. 'You have no idea, Paul Seton. Sky is the one who led me to believe. She is one of the most Godly people I've ever met.'

'Oh, Kathina,' Paul said, coming to her and putting an arm around her. 'You always see the best in people. It's in your nature. You're just so sweet and loving that—'

Kathina shook his arm off and stepped back to glare at him. 'Stop feeling sorry for me, Paul. Stop being nice because you see me as someone lesser than you; someone in need of your help. I don't need your flattery. I know who I am, what I look like. And Sky treats me as an equal, as competition as you put it, because she values and respects me the way I am. That's more than I can say about you!'

'Kathina!' Paul's voice came out hoarse and shocked. 'That's not true. I do like you. Truly. Just the way you are.'

She turned away. 'Well that's a pity, because that's more than I can say about you right now. In fact, I don't even know who you are anymore.'

Paul studied her for a few moments, glanced at Alexa and Joanna, then left the kitchen. Sky left out the other door.

Chapter Sixteen

Sky felt the full force of Paul's rejection. Yet she knew she deserved it. No wonder her father never answered her letters and emails when she was younger. She'd told him all about her achievements, hoping he would be impressed. None of them meant anything to her unless her father cared. Unless her father was proud, she couldn't be proud of them. So she did everything within her power to impress him. She strove to always be the best, the nicest, the prettiest, the most popular. But it didn't help the awful ache inside and so she withdrew and became a troubled, spiteful child.

Until the camp when Jake explained to her that her worth didn't depend on what she achieved. It didn't even depend on what her father thought of her. It depended on God and God saw her as his own special child … as a princess.

That day had brought about great changes in her life. And yet still, deep down, there was that longing for her father to love her. For how could she truly understand her Heavenly Father's love until she knew the love of her own father?

***

Paul's mind wouldn't settle. He was about to lead the study he'd hoped to use to show Sky how wrong she was to be angry with her father. It was once again about the 'Father's love' and they would all be asked to share stories of their own father. Paul knew Sky's father better than Sky herself. For it was her father, who had supposedly abandoned her, that he'd claimed as his own for over ten years.

Paul thought back to the letters and emails Sky had sent over the years. They disgusted him. All the girl could seem to do was boast of her achievements. Unashamedly, she wrote of her success over others in gymnastics, how she topped the class in every subject, how her swimming skills were way above average and how everyone in her class looked up to her and wanted to be like her. Sky Clements was the type of girl he had trouble liking. She was clearly the type of girl who took pleasure in pulling others down and would not be happy until she was recognised as best. Her pride made it hard for him to even look at her.

To his satisfaction, Sky was subdued as the group gathered around for the study. Finally, he'd gotten through to her that she wasn't the most loveable creature on the face of the earth. His rejection of her romantic advances had penetrated the attractive surface and reached her heart. There was nothing worse than trying to put someone off and find that instead, the person just tried harder because they were so arrogant they couldn't believe you didn't want them.

'We've been talking about our perfect Heavenly Father,' Paul began by saying. 'This session we're going to be looking at the difference between our human, earthly fathers who let us down, and our perfect Heavenly Father who will never leave or forsake us. Who wants to begin?'

Normally Sky would have jumped in, but today she said nothing. She didn't even look at him.

'Alright, I'll start,' Paul looked around at them. 'Like all of you, my real father let me down, but I don't hold it against him. He dedicated me to God before his whole church. He promised he would be there to teach about God, to love and nurture me. Then he left me.'

There was absolute silence until Sky spoke in a quiet, almost timid voice. 'He didn't keep that promise?'

'No. He died when I was a baby.'

Sky's dark eyes took on a look of recognition. 'He couldn't help it, then.'

Immediately Paul jumped on the comment. 'And who says your father could? Things happen.' He shook his head, his eyes boring into hers. 'If I had my father here now, there is no way I'd be refusing to forgive him for some broken promise of the past. Your problem, Sky Clements, is that you take everyone and everything for granted. You've had exactly what you've wanted all your life. So when one person doesn't bow to your every wish, you can't forgive him.'

***

Sky's throat hurt from holding in tears. Paul had no idea of how many nights as a child she had gazed at the photo of her father and begged him to come and get her. He had no idea of the way his lack of interest in her had made her feel so unloved. After all, if her own father didn't care about her, how could she truly be of worth?

'You don't know what you're talking about, Paul,' she said quietly.

He chuckled. 'Don't under estimate me, Sky. I'm a lot more intelligent than you think and believe it or not, I may even rival your intelligence. Take my word for it, I know what I'm talking about. If you were as smart as you think you are you would have worked out who I am by now.'

Sky stared at him. 'So who are you?'

He gave a twisted grin. 'See if this helps. My adopted father is a man who has made many mistakes in his lifetime.' He gazed around at the group, glancing at Sky for just a moment. 'But he's a godly, humble man with amazing gifts. I've never met anyone like him and I'm proud to call him Dad.' He looked directly at

92

Sky, then. 'You'd be proud to call him your dad too, if you made the effort to get to know him.'

What was he talking about? His riddles were confusing her. Why would she want to meet Paul's dad? He was just making a point again. She wished he'd stop rubbing her pain over her father in her face.

***

Jake watched Sky walk toward her cabin, shoulders slumped. He'd had enough. Paul was playing games with her mind and emotions and it was wrong. He shouldn't have kept the secret this long.

'Sky?' She turned with a smile at his voice, but there was no sparkle. 'I need to talk to you.'

Her face fell. 'What have I done?'

'It's not you. Can we sit?'

She looked uncertain as she moved to the bench seat outside the cabins. He wished he could take the fear and hurt from her eyes. She bit her lip. 'Jake, do you think I'm a flirt?'

What? Where had that come from? 'No.'

Of course she wasn't. She didn't need to be. She'd never had to seek anyone's attention before. She simply had it.

'It's okay. You can tell me.' Her eyes were searching his. 'Maybe God's teaching me a lesson. Maybe Paul is the only one discerning enough to see what's in my heart. He sees how shallow I really am and that's why he hates me.'

Clearly, Paul's rejection had cut her deep. Jake sighed. 'Sky, there's something you need to know.'

Her eyes widened and he wished he could take the fear he saw there. *God, give me the words.*

'Sky, your father is Paul Seton's adopted dad. Prince is also fostering Joanna and Alexa.'

Her mouth dropped open. He could see her mind working, her expressive face showing every thought as it fell into place.

Finally, she shook her head. 'So that's why Paul's so angry that I won't forgive Prince. That's why he said I shouldn't judge until I meet him. Paul's adopted father is my dad!' Tear filled her eyes as she dropped her face into her hands. 'But he took Paul in as his own. He came for Paul.'

Jake tried to move the hands from her eyes, but she was crying properly now. 'He loves Paul.'

'Sky?' Jake knew his voice was desperate, pleading.

'Jake I'm such an idiot. When I first saw him I knew there was something about him. I thought … oh no, I can't believe I thought …'

What had she thought? Jake watched as she shook her head and broken sobs wrenched from her. 'That feeling. It was only because I've seen him before. Years ago. I was probably only four, but that's what God was trying to tell me. I knew him, that's all.' She jumped up and ran toward the girls' amenities. Jake looked around helplessly. To his relief, Kathina had seen and had followed her. He watched the door slam behind them and wished he could be there for Sky. Instead, he buried his head in his hands and prayed for her.

***

Sky was going to be sick.

'Sky?'

She heard Kathina's worried voice but couldn't move. The girl's gentle hands pushed the hair back from her face. Sky moved back from the toilet bowl dazed, her head spinning.

She turned to see her compassionate eyes. 'Jake told you, didn't he?'

Sky nodded weakly, trying to understand. 'But he's Paul Seton.'

'Yes, he kept his last name. His sister, Rachel Seton, married Prince. And they have twins—Seton and Blythe. And then there's Philippa.'

Sky moaned. 'And the first thing I said when I met Paul was that Seton and Blythe were ridiculous names. No wonder he hates me.'

Kathina shook her head. 'Don't say that. He has no reason and no right to hate you. I don't know why he's acting the way he is, but I'm sick of it and I'm not going to put up with it anymore.'

Sky looked into the girl's sweet face. 'Don't throw away an amazing friendship for me.'

She laughed and it came out kind of hollow. 'I'm not, Sky. Well, not totally. I have to admit I don't like Paul very much right now. He's acting like a different person. The caring, mature Christian from home has completely changed.'

'And I did that to him.' Sky began to cry. 'I made him into a monster because I refused to forgive my dad.'

'Stop it!' Kathina insisted. 'You didn't make him do anything. He can make his own choices. He's a big boy.'

Sky just continued to cry, moved by the way tears begin to fill Kathina's eyes too. She had the softest heart of any girl she'd ever known. 'Why didn't anyone tell me?'

'I so badly wanted to, but Paul told me not to. Even Charles and Marion said not to tell you yet. They realised as soon as they heard the name, Clements. And Prince wanted to keep it a surprise.

'A surprise?' Sky's tears finally eased as she looked into Kathina's eyes. 'Keep what a surprise?'

'Sky, there's something else you need to know.'

Scared by her serious tone, Sky sat completely still, waiting.

'Paul's family are thinking of working here at the centre. I told them about how the camp needs more attractions and were thinking of taking on horses. And Prince, your dad, is coming in a couple of days to teach us how to ride horses.'

'He's coming here?'

Kathina nodded and now Sky felt as though her heart was

going to beat out of her chest. What was she going to do?

Forgive, a quiet voice said in her heart.

'Then help me, God,' she whispered, knowing he would.

***

Jake paced the oval, watching the door to the girls' toilets. Everything in him wanted to charge in there and go to Sky. But he'd broken the rules at a camp many years ago and learned his lesson. Sky teased him, but she didn't understand that rules were made to protect campers and breaking them could cost a life.

Joanna walked past and he drew in a deep breath. The girl's expression reminded him so much of Logan. The flash of hatred he saw every now and then; the hard, set expression as she quietly watched everyone as though working out their weaknesses. She reminded him of a snake waiting to strike. Just like Logan.

His eyes slid shut as memories overwhelmed him. Logan had seemed quiet at first. But when he convinced the cabin to break the rules and go for a midnight swim, no one had imagined what he had in mind. Jake had stood in shock as Logan held one of the other boys under the water until bubbles rose to the surface. He'd jumped on him, trying to pull him back, but not before the boy had fallen unconscious.

Revenge, Logan had said. The boy was the son of his father's girlfriend. He'd planned to make it look like an accident.

Jealousy was a horrible thing. He rubbed the back of his neck. Was he jealous of Paul? Was he paranoid about Joanna? He didn't want to make Sky unnecessarily wary, but maybe he needed to say more than just reminding her to be careful.

Or maybe he just needed to leave it in God's hands. With a sigh, he sat beneath the old elm tree.

Lord, protect her, comfort her, and give me peace about it all.

Chapter Seventeen

'Starre, Regal Zion's owner is here to see him.'

Starre's hand stilled on the computer mouse, her mind suddenly far from the records she was entering for the cat brought in that morning. 'You mean he's here at the centre?'

Bruce smiled. 'Yes. In the reception area. I said I'd get you to take him to Regal Zion.'

Starre immediately thought of Chase's walker. She would need to bring Regal Zion to him.

As she rounded the corner from the reception area, she saw him. His face broke into a wide smile. Impulse overcame her and before she had thought about it, she gave him a fierce hug. 'Chase! This is a surprise!'

He pointed down at his leg. 'Look. No walker.'

She stepped back to look down. His knee had a heavy brace but was she imagining it or did his leg look stronger, the muscles no longer quite so wasted? Her face warmed as she realised she was studying his legs.

When she met his eyes, they twinkled. 'I've been exercising. Jo and the physio have been working me hard.'

She nodded. 'I can see. So you want to see Regal Zion?'

His expression turned tender. 'Not just Regal Zion. I might have hoped to see you too.'

Suddenly she was aware of Bruce standing to the side,

listening. She glanced at him and he quirked a brow. Her eyes shot back to Chase.

'How is Courtney?' She knew her question sounded pointed and wondered if Chase would take offence.

However, he just gave her a knowing smile and took her arm. 'Take me to see Regal Zion. Please.'

She laughed at his whiny 'please', knowing he had done it on purpose. Enjoying the feel of his arm on hers, she began to walk toward the door. To her surprise, he kept up easily.

'The brace supports my knee where the neuropathy affected it.' He tilted his head. 'I presume you know what neuropathy is?'

She nodded. 'We had a donkey with it. Nerve dysfunction. Causes loss of feeling and strength.'

She concentrated on the grass at their feet as they walked, making sure she avoided the uneven patches of ground.

Regal Zion seemed to sense Chase was coming and before they reached him he was running up and down the fence, snorting and letting out whinnies of delight.

'He's looking good.' Chase's voice was even, but Starre saw the way his eyes shone with joy. She took the comment as a compliment. She'd brought him back to health.

Chase tried to inspect Regal Zion's legs, but the horse was too busy rubbing his face against Chase's chest and shoulder. Starre couldn't help laughing at his antics. Warmth and joy filled her heart and the feeling surprised her. It was a long time since she had felt this way.

'So what's going on with Courtney?' Starre asked the question quietly, but Chase heard her.

He continued rubbing his hand down Regal Zion's back leg, checking the healing. 'She's had enough. She's moved out.'

It was the answer she'd hoped for, yet she felt for Chase's pain at the same time.

'She won't forgive you for the accident? For … for not being able to have kids?'

He lowered Regal Zion's hoof to the ground and met her gaze. 'She's forgiven me but she can't live with it.'

Starre screwed up her face. 'That's not forgiving, is it?'

Chase came to her and his grey eyes were intense, seeming to read into her soul. 'Do you think you've forgiven me for how I treated you all those years ago?'

'Of course. When you explained what really happened I understood. You were under a lot of pressure from your dad.' She licked her lips, feeling how dry they had suddenly become.

'Starre, that's not forgiving. That's understanding.'

'Huh?'

'The chaplain explained a lot of things to me, and forgiveness was one of them.'

She wiped sweaty palms down her shorts, her mind and heart racing. 'Explain it to me?'

He looked around. 'Is there somewhere we can sit down?'

Of course. He would be getting tired, standing for so long with his injured leg. She couldn't invite him to sit on the ground.

'Hang on.' She grabbed an empty drum and upturned it for him. Then she lowered herself onto the ground. She sat, waiting expectantly as he lowered himself onto the drum. Through her mind flashed a picture she had seen in one of Blaze's Bibles. Mary sitting at the feet of Jesus, just enjoying his presence, learning from him. She felt like Mary, waiting to hear the truths of God.

'Understanding or making excuses for someone's behaviour or actions isn't forgiving them. You've heard my side of what I was going through and understood why I did what I did.'

She nodded, waiting for him to go on.

'For years you were still upset with me, still hurting, holding it against me. True forgiveness would have been if you could have let it go before you understood.'

Starre bit her lip. 'I couldn't, Chase. I tried, but I couldn't. It hurt too much.'

His Adam's apple moved and she looked up into his scarred face. 'I know and I'm sorry.'

She touched his arm. 'So what is true forgiveness?'

'It's acknowledging that someone has done the wrong thing and not met the standard they should have, but letting it go. Not holding it against them or expecting them to pay for it.'

Starre gazed up at him. Was that humanly possible? If it was, why hadn't she been able to do it? 'Have you been able to forgive anyone like that?'

His eyes slid shut for a moment. 'Not until a few weeks ago. I was talking to the chaplain about Dad. I was able to forgive him. And it set me free. I know I'll probably never run or dance again, but it's like my spirit is dancing for joy inside me.'

She knew he spoke the truth. He'd opened his eyes again and they sparkled with life. 'It changed you.'

He nodded. 'Yes.'

'So forgiving is humanly possible.'

He smiled and tucked a wisp of her hair behind her ear. 'No. But with God, nothing is impossible. The chaplain explained to me about Jesus forgiving me for not meeting God's standards. How he died for me before I even knew he existed; before I was born. It's only when we know and understand Jesus' love for us and how much he has forgiven us, that we can pass that same forgiveness on to other people.'

Starre's heart and mind raced. His words made sense. If only she could have forgiven Chase whether she understood his actions or not. If only she could have let it go, she might not have suffered all these years, trapped in her own prison of pain, knowing she had been wronged and putting up walls to stop it even happening again.

She jumped to her feet. 'Oh, Chase.' Her eyes filled with tears.

He stood too, unsteadily at first, but then he took both her hands, holding her in front of him.

'I did wrong by you, Starre. I put caring for Sky before you. I put pleasing my dad in front of you. I sacrificed our relationship. No excuses. I made the wrong choice and you've suffered for years. Will you forgive me because God forgives me?'

She choked on a cry. *God, forgive me for being so stubborn, for holding this against Chase, for shutting out Blaze, for being jealous of Sky. For holding myself back from knowing you and believing in your love and forgiveness. I've wasted so many years when I could have really been living!*

Her eyes locked with Chase's. 'I forgive you.'

***

Sky didn't sleep well. Her dreams were filled with visions of her mother drawing her last breath. Then she dreamed she was watching her father fall from the back of a horse. Every time he ended up in a broken, crumpled heap on the ground and she was trying to tell him she really did love him. Then she saw Paul. He was laughing at her; a grating, mocking laugh.

She awoke with a start. Pain knotted in a ball in her stomach.

'You okay?'

Alexa was awake, studying her. Sky pulled herself together. 'Yes. Just a rough night.'

'You were moaning in your sleep.'

'Oh. Sorry.' She jumped up and grabbed her toiletries. She needed a good shower. She needed to escape Alexa's probing eyes. It was as though a lifetime of anguish had been opened up overnight and she couldn't think straight. Everything hurt. She managed to get through breakfast, vaguely aware of Kathina and Adelle trying to draw her out and check she was okay.

The whole camp was heading down to the pool to swim that morning, but for the first time in her life Sky didn't feel like going. Lost and troubled, she made her way to the kitchen to find Marion and Charles. They might be able to help her make sense of all that was going on in her heart and mind.

However, as she came through the doorway she saw Marion's strained expression and the way she looked helplessly around at the pile of breakfast pots and pans on the stainless steel bench. Now wasn't the time to unleash her own burdens. 'You look exhausted.'

Marion looked at her and smiled a tired smile. 'I am. We have some people coming tomorrow to check out the camp centre and I want to get the place cleaned up a bit.'

Sky studied her, hoping she would admit it was her father coming. But clearly she had always been so negative about her father no one was willing to be open and honest with her. That hurt more than anything.

Marion rubbed her eyes and glanced toward where Charles was loading the camp dishwasher. What Marion and Charles really needed was a morning off.

'Why don't you go swimming with the rest of them?' Sky asked, taking the washing up brush from Marion's hands.

Marion gave a grateful smile. 'Thanks, but no thanks, Sky. You love swimming. We all know that.'

Sky thought of the bikini she had talked Bonnie into buying for her. She had looked forward to diving and showing off her skill. But it didn't matter anymore. She couldn't bear the thought of anyone admiring her in that bikini. She didn't deserve to be admired. She didn't even deserve to be loved. 'Well at least let me help you, then,'

Marion met Sky's dark eyes. 'Are you okay?'

Sky gave a dry laugh. 'Am I usually so selfish that you can't believe I want to help you now?'

Marion looked shocked. 'Of course not!' She put an arm around Sky and gave her a quick squeeze. 'I just know how much you love swimming. But if you want to help me, I'd love your company.'

Sky brightened and began scrubbing the dishes. As they worked, Marion shared with Sky her concerns about the campsite. She was hoping that the new family would make all the difference and that the horses would draw in more camps.

'Marion, I know who's coming.'

She stiffened and Sky made herself smile as she continued scrubbing the pot in her hands. 'It's okay. I know why you didn't tell me.'

Marion still looked shell-shocked and Sky sighed. She let the pot fall into the water and faced Marion. 'I do wish you'd told me, though. I would have been a bit more careful what I said about my dad. I wouldn't have been negative about him in front of Paul.'

Still, she didn't seem to know what to say. She opened and shut her mouth a few times. Sky picked up the pot again and scrubbed viciously at a burnt spot on the bottom. 'There's tension in our study group because Paul's so angry with me for not forgiving my father. His father.'

Marion let out a slow breath. 'Oh, Sky. I'm so sorry. That's why he's been so awful to you. I really couldn't understand that. Charles thought it was because he's attracted to you and doesn't know how to deal with it.'

'No,' she said with a dry smile. 'He really does hate me.'

Marion's eyes widened. 'Hate is a strong word. It's my guess that Paul will soon realise who you really are and his feelings for you are going to do an about turn.'

Sky didn't respond, but she doubted it.

'You know, we're pretty much finished, way before lunch time,' Marion said after the sandwiches were made and the kitchen tidied.

'What about the knives and boards and things we used?'

'Those are for the guys on after lunch pot-wash.'

Sky shrugged. 'I'll do them. I'm sure they won't mind.'

She'd just begun when Adelle danced into the kitchen. 'Sky,

what do you think you're doing? You missed out on swimming.'

Sky simply nodded and Adelle looked at her closely. 'You can't let him get to you like this, Sky.'

Sky didn't answer. Was Paul getting to her or was she facing the truth for the first time in her life—that Sky Clements on her own was nothing. She had no right to be angry with her father for not being a father to her when God himself had adopted her. God loved her because he made her, not because she was so good at gymnastics and the best swimmer in her school, not because she was intelligent and beautiful. He just loved her.

***

Paul was surprised when his group arrived for pot-wash duty to find there was nothing left to wash. 'What happened? Where are the pots?'

Adelle was walking past and heard his question. 'Sky did them.'

Paul frowned. 'That'd be right. Just trying to make me feel guilty …'

'No!' Adelle said with such intensity that Paul was surprised. 'Paul, she didn't even know you were on pot-wash. I'm sure she never meant for anyone to find out.'

She shook her head at Paul's dubious look. 'You think you know her, Paul Seton, but you've really got no idea. You disgust me!'

Paul frowned. 'No, she's not who you think she is. I know about her; about her attitude to her father. He's my father!'

'For someone who's so wrapped up in this forgiveness issue, you'd think you'd be able to forgive her for not forgiving her father,' Adelle said.

'But she's not sorry. She just keeps holding on to the bitterness and making my dad miserable.'

'And is forgiveness about being sorry? Didn't Christ die for us while we were still sinners, before we even thought

104

of saying sorry? Forgiveness as I see it is about seeing that people don't meet up to our standards, but just letting it go. Forgiveness fills in the gap between our expectations and what their actions actually were.'

Paul grinned. 'Couldn't have said it better myself.'

'So?'

'So what?'

'So are you going to forgive Sky for not meeting your expectations of what a daughter should do when her father suddenly decides he wants her after all?'

Paul didn't answer and Adelle glared at him. 'Sky has changed from the happy girl I know and it's all your fault!'

Paul shrugged and moved out into the hall. Trust Adelle to come to Sky's defence. Sky had her under her spell too. Why was he the only one who could see her arrogance? Why was everyone so keen to feed her pride and let her think she was wonderful?

With a sigh, he moved to where Kathina was setting the table for lunch. He came to put an arm around her in his usual, friendly way, but she moved from his touch. Surprised, he studied her. 'Are you still upset with me over the Sky thing?'

She blushed. 'I just don't want you hugging me right now.'

'Why?'

She moved to put some knives on the table. 'Maybe I am still a bit annoyed with you.'

'Why?' Paul felt irritation rise up within. 'Because I'm not in love with your friend who is so popular she can have anyone she wants?'

'Paul!'

'It's true. She puts on her "I'm so beautiful and confident" act and dances around like she expects all creation to fall at her feet.'

'So Sky might use her popularity and personality to her advantage.' Kathina paused in her table setting again and her eyes bored into his. 'But hasn't it occurred to you that you use your popularity in a far worse way?'

'What do you mean by that?'

'She uses hers to develop relationships. To make friends. You use yours to hurt. To tear down those you despise. You have become one of the most spiteful, jealous people I have ever known and I don't know how to deal with it.'

Paul stood to his full height. 'I'm not jealous of her.'

'Then what is it?' Kathina pointed a fork at his chest. 'No. Don't bother trying to explain. Whatever you say, there's no excuse for your behaviour.'

Perplexed, Paul watched her walk away. Why did Kathina Davies love Sky Clements so much? And why did it hurt to have her so angry with him? Maybe in some ways he was like Sky; used to everyone liking and respecting him. He wasn't used to anyone being so upset with him. For just a moment he had a taste of what perhaps Sky was feeling.

Chapter Eighteen

Starre finished checking Regal Zion's wounds before looking up at Chase. 'I need to see Sky.'

He didn't seem surprised by her blurted comment, but his eyes searched hers. 'Why?'

She shrugged. 'I don't even know if I can explain. But can you come with me?'

He smiled. 'Do you think you should talk to Blaze and Bonnie about it first?'

Starre bit her lip to hold back her smile. 'Always the rational, sensible one, aren't you?'

He grinned. 'Always the reckless, impulsive one, aren't you?'

Her smile faded. 'Once I was, yes. Not these days, though.'

'I don't know.' He reached a hand to tuck her hair behind her ear. 'I think we might see some of the old Starre return now you've been set free to be you again.'

Set free. He'd described how it felt perfectly. His look was so intense and his eyes had dropped to her lips. She stepped back, memories flooding her mind of the last time he'd kissed her. She'd melted into him, believing she was in love; that nothing could come between them. How wrong she'd been. But forgiveness would let go of that. Give him a second chance. She moved closer, but he stopped her, putting his hands on her shoulders.

'I've been thinking we should tell Prince we have Regal Zion.'

'We?'

He smiled but didn't answer. She sighed. He was right. They should. But what if Prince asked for him back? Would Chase let him take him?

'I'm allowed out of rehab for a few days. How about we visit Sky? Then later, when I'm better and Regal Zion's up to travelling, let's take him to visit Prince. See how they respond to each other. Then we'll decide.'

'You mean just pack our things today and go and visit Sky?'

'After we've spoken to Blaze and Bonnie, of course.'

Starre grinned at him. 'Of course.'

***

The Clements family had arrived at the camp. Excitement buzzed through the cabins as each group prepared to go horse riding. Sky loved horses, but she didn't want to go horse riding yet. She wasn't ready to meet Prince.

'Please,' Joanna and Kathina pleaded with her. 'We'll go with Paul's group. Then you don't have to see your dad.'

Sky hesitated. Joanna hadn't asked her to do anything before. And Paul was only teaching them the basics. She would fit into that group. As much as she loved horses, she'd never ridden one before.

But facing Paul made her feel sick. 'I don't think I can.'

'If you're worried about Paul picking on you, don't. I'll stick by you,' Kathina promised, then gritted her teeth, 'If he dares make one comment …'

Sky took a deep breath and agreed to come. She had to face Paul sooner or later.

The sight of the horses lined up along the fence buoyed her spirits. They truly were the most beautiful creatures she could imagine. Paul was saddling one, his actions smooth and confident. The horse clearly loved him and responded to his voice, turning its head in his direction and patiently waiting for him to finish.

'He's amazing with horses,' Kathina said in her ear, 'but you've never seen anything like his father ...' she cleared her throat, 'I mean, your father, on a horse. And Philippa is pretty amazing too.' She studied Sky for a moment. 'You look so much like Philippa I don't know why it never occurred to me that you were related. And the twins look a bit like you too, though not quite as much.'

'When did you realise?'

'After last camp. But Paul asked me not to tell you. He said you were upset with your dad and it would be better you didn't know. I'm sorry I never said anything.'

Sky felt shame fill her. She'd never made an effort or asked to meet her half-brother and sisters. She'd seen photos of when they were younger, but she'd refused to let herself really take any notice of them. It hurt too much to know her father had other children he wanted; other children he kept.

Kathina stopped talking as Paul began giving instructions in his deep, mellow voice. Campers lined up, one by one, to be assisted onto the horses. Sky tried to find a way out of it, but found herself carried along in the line with everyone else.

It was Jake's turn and he was able to climb onto the horse without Paul's help. Sky felt relief. She should be able to do that too. She didn't think she could handle Paul's touch right now. She watched as Paul directed the group, leading each horse in turn and helping those who were struggling.

Jake leapt from his horse and came to her with a grin. 'So, horse girl, here's your chance to show us what you can do.'

Sky attempted a smile at him. 'I can't do anything. I've only been on a horse a few times before.'

Jake's eyes widened in pretend horror. 'What? You mean you can't leap onto the horse's back and do all kinds of amazing acrobatics like you do in the pool?'

Sky's eyes misted over. 'Like my dad can?'

'Oh, Sky.' Jake's voice was deep with emotion as his arm

came around her. 'I'm so sorry no one told you.' His eyes darkened with anger. 'I still think they should have!'

Sky swallowed hard. 'But they know how much trouble I've had forgiving Dad. Maybe they expected me to throw a tantrum or something.'

Jake let out a low laugh. 'I've never seen you throw a tantrum. I wouldn't mind seeing it, though.'

She shook her head and sighed. 'I've been throwing a tantrum of unforgiveness for years.'

He frowned. 'You think so?'

'Yes. Stupid, I know.'

'Not stupid. Understandable. I know you'll do the right thing, Sky. You have an amazing heart for God and I know you'll listen as he directs you from here.'

He gave her a final squeeze. She looked up into his eyes and smiled her first full, complete smile all day. 'Thanks Jake. I needed that.'

She pulled back to see Paul glaring in her direction. 'Sky! You're up. We're waiting!'

The impatience in his tone jarred her, but Jake leaned close. 'Don't let the way others treat you make you forget how special you are, Sky,' he said in a low voice before moving aside.

Sky threw him a smile before coming to Paul where he stood by the large horse. He moved his mouth close to her ear.

'Well, I see you're really distressed by the fact that I don't return your love. Glad you've found someone else to shower your affections on, though.'

Sky bit her lip to stop it trembling. She willed the tears she felt coming to stop. They were threatening and so to get away, she turned from Paul and tried to leap onto the back of the horse. To her horror, it threw up its legs and kicked. She found herself on the ground, while Paul attempted to settle the creature.

Painfully, she stood.

'What do you think you were doing?' Paul's voice was loud enough for everyone to hear. 'You never jump onto a horse out of the blue like that. And what were you trying to do? Jump on its tail? The middle of the horse is here!' He jabbed his finger at the saddle.' He moved in closer. 'If you'd just let Dad teach you to ride in the first place you wouldn't have made a fool of yourself in front of everyone like this!'

Unwanted tears sprang to her eyes. 'Don't you think you've humiliated me enough?'

Paul shook his head in disgust. 'You're such a performer, Sky Clements!'

Sky turned and fled, unable to hold back her sobs. Blindly, she raced to the kitchen.

Marion was in there, peeling carrots, and she turned in surprise to see Sky. 'What's wrong?' She rushed to enfold Sky in her arms.

'I need to go home.'

'Sky, what happened?' Marion smoothed Sky's hair, trying to calm her down.

'I'm no good at being a leader. My own life's a mess!'

'But Sky, you've been doing a great job! None of us are perfect!'

But Sky shook her head against Marion's comforting shoulder. 'I can't do it. I just can't!'

Marion stiffened and Sky looked up and followed her gaze. Paul was standing in the doorway.

'Let me speak to her. In private?'

Sky shook her head, no, but to her horror, Marion walked out the door.

'Please don't!' Sky stepped back, unable to look at him and still unable to hold back her tears. 'I can't take any more.'

When Paul said nothing, she dared look up. He was rubbing his forehead, his expression perplexed.

'Sky, I'm sorry.' His voice sounded hoarse. 'I went too far. I told myself I'd stop it once Kathina told me off, but it kind of became a habit.'

She couldn't answer. He only cared what he'd done because he cared what Kathina thought. It occurred to her then that maybe he really did have feelings for her.

'Sky, I'm your brother's and sister's uncle,' Paul said, his eyes imploring her to believe him.

She drew in a deep, shuddering breath but the tears continued to stream down her face. 'I know.'

He looked surprised, but continued. 'So we both know all about having a father who sinned, but we also know about forgiveness. I have forgiven him for his past mistakes.'

Sky nodded. 'Because he fathered you, Paul. You're not even his own son and he managed to be your father. You've never had someone leave simply because they don't want you.'

Paul looked like he was about to defend Prince again, but Sky cut him off. 'You don't understand.'

A bemused look came across his face. 'Yes, that's what Jake just told me while giving me a good tongue lashing.' His shoulders lifted. 'So make me understand.'

She simply stared at him.

'Please. I'll try to listen.'

Sky lowered herself onto one of the kitchen stools and Paul did the same.

'He gave me a picture of him when I was about three.' Sky tried to hold her voice steady. 'He just handed it to me and then ran off. Until then I didn't even know I had a father. Then he wrote me another letter when I was four. He promised to come and visit me soon and someday I would have the choice of joining his family.'

Paul raised his brows. 'And he never gave you that choice?'

'He didn't even come to visit me. He didn't invite me to his wedding. I haven't seen him since I was three. I would write letters but he never even answered.'

'But he talked about you all the time. Didn't he ever come

and visit?'

'Not once. Then two years ago Blaze and Bonnie told me he offered to adopt me. I don't even know him!'

Paul said nothing, but Sky saw the uncertainty in his eyes.

'Everything I did, everything I achieved, it was to try to make him love me; to be proud of me and to want me. It never worked.' Her voice broke again and she shook her head. 'I know I need to forgive him. But what if he does it again? What if I get to know him and then he ignores me again? And how can I really be loveable if my own father doesn't love me?'

'He does love you, Sky. I know he does.'

'Has he told you that? He's never shown it! True love is shown in actions.'

Paul stood and held out his hands to her, but she didn't take them.

'I'm sorry,' he said again, this time awkwardly as he pulled his hands back. 'Kathina said I didn't know the full story. She was right.'

'Paul, you don't know the half of it,' Sky whispered through tears.

His brown eyes met hers in a gentle way. 'So tell me.'

She shook her head. 'I can't right now. Please just give me some space.'

With a helpless shrug, Paul left. Sky sat staring at nothing for a long time, her heart in turmoil. Paul had obviously thought she was the one in the wrong. And maybe she was. Her father wanted to make amends. She needed to let him do that. She would forgive and be grateful for Bonnie and Blaze, her adoptive parents, who truly did love her. Many times they had wanted to make her officially theirs, but she hadn't been able to bring herself to do it. Now she would.

The door burst open, and Sky watched in horror as Alexa rushed to the bench and grabbed a knife. She held it up at Marion who had followed her.

Chapter Nineteen

'If Paul doesn't help me onto the horse I'll cut my wrists!' Alexa's voice was threatening as she held the knife against her wrist.

Marion gazed steadily back at her. 'I'm a nurse,' she said calmly. 'So if you do that, I'll give you first aid and take you into the hospital.'

'You can't make me—' Alexa began, but with moves so fast they could hardly be followed, Joanna was there. In a flash, she grabbed the knife from Alexa's hand and held it against the surprised girl's throat.

'Joanna!' she gasped, but Joanna moved the knife closer so that the pressure of the blade was against Alexa's neck.

'You have no idea, do you, Alexa?' Joanna demanded through clenched teeth. 'You talk about death so lightly, but you'd never really kill yourself. You're all talk. But I could do it for you. I've seen a slashed throat, and it was my mother's; a person I loved. But I didn't cry, I just looked at it because I did it. How much more do you think I could kill someone I don't love?'

Sky saw Alexa swallow, her eyes showing her terror. 'Joanna,' Sky began, but Joanna cut her off.

'You're too clever, aren't you, Sky Clements!' she said coldly. 'You and all your talk about our loving God giving his life for us. You said you would like to think you would be like him and give your life for others,' she gave a sarcastic laugh. 'But you can't even forgive Prince, so it's not like you would give your life for his foster daughter, would you?'

Sky's mind worked fast. Would she? Could she really? She stared hard at the knife at Alexa's throat and Joanna let out a harsh laugh.

'I knew it! You're all talk too, Sky Clements.'

'I would do it,' Sky said so softly, it could hardly be heard. 'If you let Alex go, I will take her place.'

'As if!' Joanna sneered, and Sky gulped as she saw a small trickle of blood run slowly down Alexa's neck. The knife was beginning to cut into her.

'Just give me a chance,' Sky said quietly, amazed at how calm her own voice sounded when she was shaking so badly.

'I know you!' Joanna growled, shaking her head. 'You're just biding time to work out how to get me to drop the knife.'

'I'm not,' Sky promised. 'I'll come up close, really slowly. I'll hold my hands above my head.'

'No, get Marion to tie them. But if you try any kind of trick, this knife goes into her neck.'

'Okay.' Sky glanced to where Joanna was looking and saw the rope in the tool box Charles had left under the bench. 'Marion, tie me.'

Marion stared, her face pale. 'No, Sky.'

'Please, Marion.'

Marion's eyes pierced Sky's for a moment before she relented. She couldn't stop the tears running down her face. Sky heard her muttering a prayer, begging God for help as she tied Sky's hands. Sky felt the older woman's hands shaking.

'It's okay, Marion.'

Marion let out a strangled sob. 'Sky, I love you like my own daughter. I'm so sorry.'

Sky showed Joanna her hands were tied, then walked toward Joanna and Alexa, her steps slow and deliberate.

As quick as lightning, Joanna let go of the crying Alexa and grabbed her. She held the knife against her throat. She felt the blade sting her skin. Joanna let out a harsh laugh.

'I should cut your pretty face, Sky. See how many friends you have then. Let you see what it feels like to be normal and not have perfect skin and a perfect smile and pretty eyes. In fact, why don't I blind you?'

Sky saw the knife point move toward her eyes and closed them to shut out the sight. She imagined what it would be like to have a scarred face; to be blinded. What would it be like to be horrific to look at? Maybe she would lose friends. But Bonnie and Blaze would still love her. And Jake. Jake wouldn't care. In that moment she knew Jake was the one true friend who looked deeper than her outward appearance; who loved her for who she truly was.

Joanna gave her a shake. 'Open your eyes!'

Sky did, and sorrow filled her as she met Joanna's eyes darkened with bitterness and hate.

'Oh, Joanna. I'm so sorry for all you've been through.' Sky felt her eyes fill with tears as Joanna's flew to hers.

'Stop your little performance. Your tears mean nothing to me.' Joanna's voice was deep and harsh, almost as though she were someone else.

Everyone tensed as the door to the kitchen opened. A woman with straight, blonde hair entered. Her warm brown eyes were fixed on Joanna.

'Rachel,' Joanna's voice returned to normal.

The woman looked so calm, as though nothing out of the ordinary was happening and in that moment Sky knew who she was. Paul's sister. Prince's wife. Joanna's foster mother.

'What's going on, Joanna?' Rachel's voice was serene, as though they were having an everyday conversation.

'I hate her, that's what. And I hate Alexa's little dramas.'

Rachel came closer. 'Well let's work through that. I hardly think knifing someone is going to help.'

Joanna's eyes narrowed. 'I thought you'd want her dead. She's your husband's love child.'

Rachel smiled, then and her eyes met Sky's. 'That's why I love her too. If you hurt her, you hurt Prince and I more than you can imagine.'

Joanna went absolutely still. Sky drew in a deep breath. *Please God, I don't really want to die yet. I know I'd be coming to be with you, but there's so much I haven't sorted out yet. I don't even know Rachel. I'd like to.*

A loud clatter came as saucepans fell to the floor. Everyone turned to where Marion stood near the pots now on the floor. Momentarily distracted, Joanna didn't see Charles fly in from the other entrance. He grabbed Joanna from behind and forced the knife from her hand. Then he forced her to the floor, pinning her there with his entire weight. She moaned, and Sky pulled at Charles shirt.

'Don't hurt her,' she pleaded. 'She's just a girl. She's already in pain.'

At her words, Charles lifted Joanna to her feet, still holding her so she could hardly move. Joanna didn't even bother to struggle. She just looked at Sky.

'My Mum wouldn't believe her boyfriend raped me,' she said through eyes still hard and empty of tears. 'The only way I could get him out of my life was to kill Mum and blame him for it.'

Sky just nodded, still in a daze.

She was still in shock when the police came and took Joanna away, Rachel by the girl's side. Her last memory was of those haunted eyes and the anguish in her heart was almost too much to bear. Slowly she turned away, and then she saw Alexa.

'Thank you,' Alexa whispered, and then Sky broke down.

'Oh Alex, please don't ever kill yourself.' For the first

time, Alexa didn't correct her name. Instead she came to Sky and held her tight.

'Please call me Lexi,' she said softly. 'That's what my mum called me.'

Sky nodded, unable to speak.

The group made statements and were debriefed before they were allowed to join the other campers. Sky felt tired, so tired, yet her heart continued to beat too fast.

She heard that Prince and Rachel had gone in the police car with Joanna and might not be back for some time. She sighed. Someone else was always the priority for her father. Even a foster daughter who'd threatened to kill his own daughter.

As she walked slowly back to her room, her heart still refused to slow down. She wished she could make it steady, but she couldn't seem to take control. Then she saw Jake running toward her.

'Sky! Are you okay?' The desperation and concern in his eyes was her undoing.

'Yes.'

His eyes looked deep into hers, his brow furrowed. She was alive, and unscarred. She still had her clear, unblemished skin and her eyesight. But even if she didn't, Jake would still look at her the same. Overwhelmed with the knowledge, she threw herself into his arms and began to sob.

'Hey, it's okay, now.' His arm came around her. 'I heard all about it. I thought there was something about Joanna. I just wish I listened to my heart and followed it up.'

Sky nodded. 'I wish I'd had your discernment and suspected something in the first place.'

Jake pushed her back from him for a moment. 'You're amazing, Sky,' he said softly. 'Don't let anyone pull you down and make you feel like you're anything less that God has made you to be.'

Sky knew he was referring to Paul and lowered her eyes.

'I mean it, Sky. There are those of us who watch you in wonder, seeing the way God's love shines out of you so much you almost glow. I know that sometimes those we most want to impress don't even seem to notice us, but perhaps we are trying to impress the wrong ones.'

Sky caught his meaning and looked at him then, seeing the earnest in his eyes.

'You're such a good friend, Jake.'

He smoothed back her hair, looking past her physical appearance and into her heart. 'You are so loved, Sky. You just can't see it. That's why you strive so hard and have such high expectations of yourself.'

The way he looked at her took her breath away. 'I see it,' she whispered. 'And you're right. God is the only one I need to please and he already loves me anyway.'

Jake smiled. 'Exactly,' Then he gave her another quick hug. 'I'm glad you're still with us!'

There was a huskiness to his voice she hadn't noticed before and it warmed her heart. For the first time she felt ready to see her father. To forgive him for his failings and to love him whether or not he showed the same love in return.

That evening Marion told the campers about the drama that had unfolded with Joanna.

'I know rumours are already going around the camp.' She looked pointedly at a few people who shuffled uncomfortably. 'I think it's better you hear the story first hand, rather than making up your own version from bits and pieces.'

Sky sat at the back, arms folded tightly across her chest. Marion had insisted she ring and tell her parents what had happened. They had wanted to race to her straight away, but Sky had managed to assure them she was fine. Yet she still shook every time she thought of that knife. And when Marion related the way she had tied Sky up, campers gasped and turned to look at her. She gave them a half smile, trying to show them everything was all right. To her surprise, someone's hands came from behind and rested securely on her shoulders. She looked back to see Jake there and took his hand and held it as she turned back to face the front. The shaking stopped.

Finally it was over, and the campers left the hall. Alexa was sitting on the seats outside, and Sky came to her side.

'No wonder Joanna was so messed up,' Alexa said into her hands. 'At least my dad didn't do *that* to me.'

Sky lowered herself onto the seat beside her. 'What did your dad say that time you told him you loved him?'

Alexa met her eyes and there was deep pain there. 'He said he never loved me. That I was the reason Mum died. I wanted some milk and we had run out. Mum was on her way to buy me some because I just wouldn't stop complaining. That's when she had the car accident.'

'Lexi, it's not your fault,' Sky began, but Alexa cut her off.

'I told him it wasn't my fault and to stop drinking and face up to the truth. Then he came at me and just wouldn't stop hitting me. He broke my jaw and three ribs. I was in hospital for ages.'

She fell silent, and Sky just stared at her, her heart breaking. 'How could anyone treat you like that?' she finally asked, then looked earnestly into the eyes before her. 'You do know it's not your fault, don't you?' she implored. 'Your Dad didn't treat you like that because you deserved it. It doesn't change your worth as a person that your father didn't see who you really are. What he did was about who he is, not who you are.'

Even as Sky spoke the words, the truth began to dawn on her and she felt tears form in her own eyes. The truth began to sink deep into her soul. She didn't have to make herself worthy of her father's love. She was significant because her Heavenly Father loved her.

'You know, you were just like Jesus when you came and took my place,' Alexa said softly. 'I could see it in your eyes. You struggled, just like Jesus did in the Garden of Gethsemane. You didn't take my place because you wanted to, but because you loved me. And as you walked toward us, I told God in my heart that I believed.'

Sky saw the sincerity in the girl's eyes and tears formed in her own. 'Oh Lexi. I'm so glad!'

Chapter Twenty

Sky couldn't sleep that night. She kept seeing Joanna's empty bed and tears would fill her eyes.

'Please help her, God,' she prayed, not knowing what else to pray. Joanna was one mixed up girl. She thought of Jake's warnings. He was so discerning, so caring.

Then she thought of Paul and her father. She looked at the clock. Five am. Would she meet her father today? How long would it take to sort things out with Joanna?

Slowly, she got up. There was no way she could sleep anymore.

She wandered across the grass in the early morning light, her heart filled with prayer.

I understand why Jake loves coming out so early and spending time with you, God. She looked up as a galah flew overhead then landed in a tree branch. *You made this world for us to enjoy. It's beautiful. So peaceful and still. It's easy to know you love me!*

'Sky?'

Sky almost jumped at the sound of Jake's voice. He sat at the base of the tree, his Bible in his lap.

'Sorry,' he grinned and his voice was throaty as though they were his first words for the day. His ginger hair, usually so neat, poked up in all directions. 'I didn't mean to scare you.'

'You're up early.'

He nodded. 'Couldn't sleep.'

'Me either.'

She sat down on the grass beside him, then chuckled. 'It's wet.'

His eyes twinkled at her. 'Yep. That's why I'm sitting on a towel.'

He moved for a moment to open the towel out further so that she could sit on it too.

Sky sat back down beside him, looking to where his Bible was opened.

'Jesus' death,' she said quietly, skimming the words.

He nodded rubbing a hand through his hair. 'Yeah. I just had to read it again. What happened to you yesterday really got me thinking.'

'About?'

He looked uncomfortable for a moment and avoided her eyes. She watched as he rubbed his chin then gave a sigh. His eyes met with hers.

'I couldn't have done what Mum did, Sky. I couldn't have tied you. I ...' he hesitated and searched her eyes. 'I love you too much. But God, our Heavenly Father, he allowed his own son to be tied, to be killed on a cross. His love for us is ..., well, it's unbellevable!'

Sky swallowed hard as tears filled her eyes. 'It is.' He was still looking at her and she couldn't tear her gaze away. 'This has been a hard camp for me, Jake. I've learned a lot about myself, my pride, my unworthiness before God.'

He nodded. 'I know. It's been so hard to watch you go through it. You've no idea how many times I wanted throttle Paul Seton!'

Sky's eyes widened. She had never thought anything could rattle the calm, placid Jake.

'Funny, isn't it?' he said. 'How we're meant to be leaders, but often it's us who learn and grow the most at these camps.'

Sky simply nodded as she looked into his open, friendly face. She knew exactly what he meant.

'So, you get to meet your father today,' he said as he rested his arms across his knees.

She nodded again. He put a hand on her arm for a moment and she wondered at how her heart beat faster.

'I'll be praying for you,' he said.

Sky looked down at his hand, then back up him. 'Thank you.'

They sat silently for a few moments, looking out across the lawn, before Sky suddenly chuckled. 'I hope you didn't really take me off your list.'

It took a moment for him to catch on, but when he did, he gave a shy smile. 'The list. You're the only one on it.'

Her eyes widened. 'You really have one?'

He grinned sheepishly. 'I used to feel guilty about it, wondering if I only had you on there because you're so … well, so attractive. But this camp has just confirmed it to me. You're even more beautiful inside than you are out. Your love of God, your humility, your—'

'Stop, Jake,' she pleaded, and he did, though his eyes still held hers.

'I've made so many mistakes, Jake. I have messed up, I'm—'

He leaned in closer and stopped her words with a gentle brush of his lips on her forehead. 'You're forgiven.'

'Yes,' she whispered breathlessly. 'Forgiven.'

Sky floated back to her cabin. Jake was an amazing young man. In fact, she admired and respected him more than any other she had met. Why had that only just become clear to her? He had been one of her closest friends for a long time. And there was something special there; something she could never have had with Paul Seton, mysterious and reserved as he was.

Adelle met her on the verandah of the cabin. 'Sky, there's a man looking for you.'

Sky's eyes widened. 'Another police officer?'

'I don't think so. That's him over there.'

Sky looked to where she pointed and saw him in the distance. He was standing near the horses. Cautiously, she approached and the stranger turned. She found herself gazing at the most handsome man she had ever seen. He was about thirty years old and there was no mistaking who he was.

He was so much like her beloved foster father Blaze, yet so different too. He stood a good six feet tall with raven black hair and a smile so friendly she couldn't help smiling in return. Then he stopped short and those intense eyes darkened to a near black. She saw the way he became apprehensive as he took a step toward her, then hesitated. 'Sky?'

Sky felt herself begin to tremble as she stood perfectly still, arms folded across her chest as though she were cold.

'Are you … is …' He seemed overcome.

Her chest tightened. Prince. Her father. She made her voice work. 'Dad?'

With a cry of joy he came to her, throwing his arms around her and giving her the hug she'd longed for all her life. Tears coursed down her cheeks, and she saw that they sparkled in his eyes too.

'Can you forgive me?' Prince Clements asked, and Sky nodded, knowing that had she met her father like this only a week ago, she wouldn't have looked at him, let alone run into his arms and held him tight. She had Paul Seton to thank for that. No, she had God.

'I can't believe I nearly lost you yesterday.' Prince's voice caught. 'I took in foster children your age, thinking that somehow it could make up for the way I abandoned you, but instead, one of them almost killed you!'

Sky stepped back and looked him in his dark eyes, asking the question she had been too scared to ask her whole life.

'Why didn't you come for me, Dad? Why didn't you even visit?'

Prince swallowed hard. 'I planned to visit. I really did. But when the twins were born there was so much going on. They were so much work and we took in a girl who was wanted by the police, and I was involved in a church I didn't realise was actually dealing drugs to the homeless. Then Rachel's grandparents died and Paul needed a home and you were doing so well with Blaze and Bonnie …' He stopped, seeming to notice Sky's expression for the first time.

'I'm your child too, Prince … Dad. I was your child first. You promised you would come and get me.'

Prince said nothing as he gazed at her, then he shook his head. 'You looked so poised and confident in all the pictures Blaze sent us. But the pictures didn't show the sadness I can see in person, Sky.' His eyes glistened. 'It hurts to know I put it there. I'm so sorry I didn't keep my promise. I'm sorry I let fear and convenience rule over loyalty and commitment. You're right. You are my child. My first born. My daughter.'

He looked so full of anguish that Sky knew it was true. He had only just realised the impact of his choices.

'I'm so sorry,' he said, 'I really am. I could give you so many reasons and excuses, but ultimately I failed you. I kidded myself you were okay because my brother had you, but you weren't, were you?'

Her eyes filled with tears as she shook her head. 'Not really.'

'Can it ever be all right?'

Sky nodded, unable to speak.

His arms came around her again and she allowed herself to be drawn in and held against his chest. His hands stroked her hair, holding her gently as though she were precious. She could hear the steady beating of his heart and something deep inside stopped hurting so badly. A part of her began to feel whole again.

They stood that way for a good five minutes before Prince pulled back, his dark eyes looking tenderly into hers. 'Is there somewhere quiet we can go to talk? To really catch up?'

Sky led him to the conference hall. It was always empty at this time of day. However, this morning it wasn't. Paul sat in one corner, quietly strumming his guitar. He stood, looking unsure as the two came into the room.

'It's okay,' Sky reassured him. 'Don't feel like you have to leave.'

'You sure?'

Prince and Sky nodded at once, and so Paul sat back down, but didn't resume his playing.

'Dad, can you tell me the reasons?' Sky pulled out two chairs. 'I've wondered for so many years.'

Prince sat down slowly, watching as she sat across from him. Sky was aware Paul had moved closer, but her eyes were fixed on her father.

'I was only sixteen when you were born.' Prince bit his lip. 'I was a circus boy with no regard for God or anyone else, really. I was also too scared to admit you were my daughter because I had no idea how to be a father. My own father had never really been there for us, and my mother died when I was so young I can't even remember her. Your mother was a circus girl, too …. still is, as far as I know.'

Sky shook her head. 'She died, Dad. Just before camp. I saw her and she said not to hold anything against you or Chase because you had no choice or something. She wanted us to tell Aunty Starre that.'

Prince's eyes took on a haunted look. 'I let her down too, Sky. I knew she was an alcoholic. I didn't try to help.'

Sky sighed. 'Do you think it would have made any difference?'

Prince's eyes raised in contemplation before his shoulders sagged. 'Probably not. But the point is, I didn't try.'

'Do you know what she meant about having no choice?'

He looked uncomfortable. 'Not sure about with Chase and Starre, but Carrie certainly put everything into seducing me. But that's no excuse. I still had a choice.'

Sky didn't know what to say. He was right. He'd done the wrong thing. But talking about it helped and it didn't hurt quite so much anymore. For the first time she felt ready and able to hear the full story.

'How did you end up marrying Rachel?'

She sensed Paul leaning closer, hanging on his father's every word. Prince seemed unaware. A light came to his dark eyes at the mention of Rachel.

'I knew Rach from school. I had a lot of respect for her. She was a Christian and had standards, but I guess I kind of liked a challenge.' He looked away, unable to meet her eyes. 'Her parents died and her boyfriend betrayed her. She was broken. And I deliberately seduced her when she was at her most vulnerable.' He licked his lips. 'It's okay. I know I deserve your disgust.'

Sky tried to hide the shock she felt. 'You didn't even love her?'

'No. I was attracted to her, though.'

'And she was a Christian?'

Prince sat up. 'Don't condemn her, Sky. She had just lost her parents. Her boyfriend had hurt her horribly, she'd failed uni and she had a little brother who needed caring for. It was wrong of her to succumb to me, but we all make mistakes.'

Sky shook her head, struggling to comprehend. It was at that point Paul stood from behind them, his eyes filled with fury. He began to speak, then stopped while Prince held his hand out to him.

'You might as well join us, Paul. You need to hear the whole story, too.'

Paul approached. Sky moved away slightly, sensing the intensity of Paul's feelings. Was he angry with her or his adopted father?

Prince didn't seem to notice Paul's reaction and continued.

'Rachel became pregnant and I became a Christian and we decided to get married.'

'Even though you didn't love her?' Paul spoke this time and his voice was low. Sky saw the way his hands shook as he clasped them together in his lap.

Prince smiled tenderly at the memory. 'I did by then. It was her concern for me, the poems and songs she wrote and all her prayers for me that led me to want to find out more about God. I learned what it is to really love someone. Not to just be attracted to them, but to respect them and want to give without wanting something in return.'

Sky swallowed hard. 'What about me?' she almost whispered. 'You said you'd come for me.'

Prince nodded. 'And I fully intended to, but I had no idea what it's like to care for one baby, let alone two. I had planned to introduce you to the twins once they arrived, but they were so much work you didn't even cross my mind until they were about two years old. Then Rachel's grandparents died and Paul came to live with us. There were so many adjustments, dealing with the twins and helping Paul get through his grief and confusion. Then Philippa was on the way.'

She leaned forward. 'Did you ever think of me?'

Prince swallowed hard. 'Sometimes. Especially when I got your letters. You seemed to be going so well. You seemed so happy with Blaze and Bonnie and I didn't know if I could continue parenting the way they did.'

'But you're my father!'

'I know.' Prince sighed. 'But not a good one.'

'You could have been.'

He shook his head. 'I don't know about that. Blaze was always a high achiever, Sky. And Bonnie too. So good at school and sport … and you seemed to be just like them. I couldn't have helped you be so good at gymnastics or diving or school'

'But Dad, I did it for you! So I could write and tell you and make you proud.' Sky's eyes filled with tears. 'I just wanted to make you want me.'

'Oh, Sky.' Prince's voice broke as he came to her and drew her into his arms, holding her close against his heart again. 'I'm so sorry, my Sky. I love you so much. When I heard what Joanna did to you I felt the same way I feel about the twins and Philippa. I felt so angry I'd failed you. And now I just feel so … so much sorrow.' He hesitated. 'Paul?'

Sky looked up. What she saw, shocked her. Paul Seton was staring at Prince in a way that made her cringe. The fury he felt was clearly expressed in his eyes.

'Do you know how I defended you, Prince?' He spoke through gritted teeth, his jaw clenched and his whole body shaking. Sky felt Prince flinch. Paul hadn't called him 'Dad'.

She stepped from her father's arms, holding her hand out to Paul. 'Paul, it's okay.'

Paul shook his head, fists clenched. 'It's not okay, Sky. I treated you like dirt because I thought my father was a godly man. I forgave him for everything he did before he was a Christian … but I had no idea!'

'Paul!'

Paul managed to stop and stare hard at Sky. Her voice expressed her anguish. 'Paul, you taught me to forgive. If you hadn't done what you did, I wouldn't love my dad the way I do now.'

Paul threw his chair behind him. 'He doesn't deserve it, Sky. You knew that all along. And now I know that too.'

'Deserve it? No one deserves forgiveness. It's a gift, remember?'

Paul just shook his head as he stormed from the room.

Sky looked to Prince, who was watching Paul leave, his face etched with regret.

'I'm sorry, Dad,' she whispered.

He shook his head. 'It's okay. We'll work it out. He just needs time.'

CHAPTER TWENTY-ONE

Jake looked across the oval, knowing he should be heading in for breakfast. But just the sight of Paul stalking from the hall made him angry. What had he been doing in the hall while Sky met with her father? Hassling her again? The guy was a bully.

Jake shook his head. If only he'd stopped Joanna from trying to hurt Sky when he could have. Well, he was going to stop Paul. Paul Seton had crossed the line.

'Paul.' He knew he sounded aggressive as he charged across the oval.

Paul looked up in surprise. 'Jacob. What can I do for you?'

Jake's eyes narrowed. 'You can stop bullying Sky.'

'Bullying?'

Jake was breathing hard, now. 'Yes.' He shoved Paul in the chest. 'What kind of man tears down a girl like that?'

Paul looked back calmly. 'I know I deserve whatever you're going to do to me, Jacob.'

The tight ball of anger in Jake's chest intensified. The guy knew no one called him by his full name. Was he just trying to provoke him further?

'The way you treat her is just wrong. She's not proud and heartless. You have no idea!'

To his surprise, Paul looked down. 'I know. I refused to forgive her for not forgiving Prince. I'm a hypocrite.'

Jake's anger completely diffused. That was not the response he expected. People were heading in for breakfast. He should be in there too.

Paul stepped back. 'Look, I'm on duty this morning. Can we finish this discussion later?'

Discussion? Guiltily, Jake acknowledged that's what it should have been. And normally he would have discussed it calmly. *God, help me. Forgive me.* He forced himself to walk into the noisy hall. Sky was already there, sitting with her cabin, minus Joanna. She was leaning toward Alexa and the two were talking animatedly. Alexa smiled and laughed at something Sky said.

Paul stood out the front and Jake followed his gaze. He was watching Sky and her table.

'Shh!' other tables told them, and realising what was going on, they fell quiet.

'Well, we've all had to wait an extra half minute for breakfast this morning,' Paul said, a hint of a smile playing about his lips. 'And earlier in the week Jake's cabin had to wait an extra half hour. It occurs to me that both of those times it was Sky Clements' fault.'

'What?' Kathina and Adelle were laughing, but Paul held up his hand.

'It also occurs to me that Sky, or members of her cabin must have broken the rules by going into the boys' cabin to change the clocks.'

'That's right!' Jake's cabin called out in delight, while Jake tried to quieten them. He didn't know what Paul was up to, but he was worried for Sky. Had he made things worse for her by challenging Paul?

Paul looked around at the campers. 'I think Sky should have to sing grace. What do you think?'

Immediately the room broke into shouts and claps and cheers. Before he knew what was happening, Sky had jumped up and escaped the room.

A boy from Jake's cabin let out a yell. 'Get her! Don't let her get away with it!'

Everyone jumped up from their tables, but Paul immediately ordered them to be seated. 'We don't need chaos. I'll get her.'

With that, he raced out the door and after Sky. Jake pointed to Adelle. 'Can you direct everyone in for breakfast? I'll be back.'

With that, he raced off after them. Sky disappeared into her cabin. Jake watched as Paul followed. He should know he wasn't allowed in the girls' cabin!

He heard Sky's voice. 'Please, Paul,' she begged, 'don't humiliate me anymore.'

She sounded near to tears, and her pleading caused a sudden, unexpected ache in his chest.

'I'm not,' Paul's voice came back. 'I'm not wanting to humiliate you, Sky, I promise. It's all in fun.'

Jake stood at the door. She was looking directly at Paul. Fear showed in her dark eyes usually so filled with life. 'But Paul, I can't sing like you.'

'But you can sing. I've heard you.

'When?'

'When you sat beside me for morning singing.'

Sky blushed. 'I've never sung alone,' she whispered. 'I can't do it.'

'Well sing with me, then.' Her confidence had crumbled in Paul's presence. Jake didn't like it but Paul didn't seem deterred.

'I'll sing with you,' he repeated. 'Come on, they won't let you get away with it now.' A teasing glint came to his eye. 'And neither will I.'

Jake interrupted, then, looking straight past Paul and into Sky's eyes. 'You okay?'

She almost smiled and with all his heart he longed that she would. 'I'm fine.'

'They're all yelling for you in there.' Jake sounded apologetic.

Paul frowned at him before reaching for Sky's arm.

'Come on, Sky. You heard Jake. They're all waiting for you.'

Sky's confidence had returned and her eyes sparkled at both of them. 'I don't think he has any right to make me do anything, Mr Rule Breaker—standing–in–the–girls'–cabin.' She pulled herself free from his grasp and looked at Jake. 'Is that right, Jake? You are both witnesses for each other that you've been in the girls' cabin. Nobody witnessed me in the boys' cabin because I was never in there. I have accomplices for that kind of thing.'

Jake looked down at his feet. He had stepped in, but only just. He grinned, then stepped back as Sky stood and made a dash for it.

A laugh bubbled from deep in Jake's throat as both he and Paul raced after her. She was fast, but Jake was faster. He swung her up into his arms. She let out a gasp and he searched her eyes. 'You okay?'

She struggled, but her beautiful eyes had turned soft, almost tender. 'Yeah. Thanks for rescuing me. But don't hurt him. God's a God of justice. He'll sort everything out.'

Jake's eyes widened. Did she know?

The campers cheered as Jake lowered her to the floor of the dining room. 'Sky doesn't need to sing grace. We have something to confess.' He looked pointedly at Paul as he came in the door behind them. Paul cleared his throat.

'Um, yes, we might have gone in the girls' cabin. So I guess that makes us even.' His eyes met Jake's. 'Are we even now, Jake?'

Jake nodded, catching Paul's meaning. 'Yes. We're even. Let's let it go shall we?'

Paul nodded and Jake looked to where Sky was joining her table again. She smiled a deep, full smile, not even looking at Paul.

Thank you, God, for your justice, but help me live out your forgiveness too.

***

135

That afternoon, Sky watched her father in amazement. He stood on the back of a cantering horse, keeping perfect balance. Then, with a back-flip he landed neatly on the ground. The watching campers cheered and clapped, unable to help themselves.

'No wonder you're such an amazing person,' a familiar voice said in her ear, and Sky turned to smile at Jake.

'He's impressive.'

Jake nodded before moving forward to organise the campers into groups for horse riding. Sky found herself constantly watching her father, and saw the way he also kept looking in her direction and smiling. He truly did care.

She was hesitant to attempt riding again but this time her father helped her onto the horse. He encouraged her until she felt confident and relaxed. The horse responded well to her and soon her love of the creatures took away any fear she had felt.

'I wish I'd let you teach me earlier,' she told Prince with regret as she dismounted and stood stroking the horse's nose. 'I could have been riding all these years!'

Prince smiled at her and pointed at the horse now nuzzling into her shoulder. 'So, will you accept her now?'

Sky's eyes widened. 'This is the horse you were offering me?'

He nodded. 'Yes. She's gentle and great for a beginner. Her name's Little Cloud.'

Sky grinned as she looked up at the large creature. 'Suits her, somehow, but I wouldn't really describe her as little.'

'You would if you saw the other horses; the ones we train for dressage.'

Sky looked from her father, to the horse, then back to her father again. 'Where would I keep her?'

'Here. We're all moving here so I can work with the horses. We're selling the dressage horses and keeping the ones that are good for trail riding. You won't be so far away any more. You can visit her any time you like … and you can visit me too.'

Sky couldn't answer for a moment. Her heart felt so full. She'd wasted so much of her energy and time on bitterness and pain. If only she'd forgiven her father and trusted God's love so much sooner.

'I'd love her,' she finally said. 'I do love her!'

Prince shrugged and handed her the reigns. 'Then she's yours. Take her for a walk. Talk to her. Get to know her.'

Sky enjoyed leading the horse—her horse—through the open gate and up into the hills. She needed time to think and walking with Little Cloud was perfect. The horse was company, but she didn't demand her attention.

Camp was almost over and so much had happened. No other camp had been so eventful, and no other had changed her so deeply.

She lost track of time. She was in her own world when a fox suddenly ran out from a bush and flashed past her. Both she and Little Cloud started. Before Sky could react, the horse had bolted forward and out of sight. She started after her, calling her name. It didn't take long for Little Cloud to disappear from sight, and in that same moment Sky realised she was lost.

Chapter Twenty-Two

Starre waited as the phone rang out again. Why weren't Blaze and Bonnie answering? She glanced at Chase. 'I think I'll just head there.'

Chase grinned. 'And be impulsive?'

She screwed up her nose at him. 'Yes.'

She started as a text came through. 'Whoa, that's loud.'

Chase chuckled. 'Well, the phone is against your ear.'

But Starre barely heard him. She scanned the text, trying to comprehend what she was reading. Then she jumped up. 'Chase, we have to go. Now.'

He put a steadying hand on her arm. 'Why? What's up?'

'A girl tried to kill her and now she's missing.'

'What? Who? What are you talking about?"

Starre drew in a deep breath. 'Blaze just texted. Sky was at a camp. Prince and Rachel are there too, and Prince's foster daughter tried to kill Sky yesterday. She was taken into custody, but now Sky's missing.'

Chase stood. 'Let's go.'

But Starre stood frozen on the spot. 'What if I've left it too late, Chase? What if I never get to see her again, to love her as my niece instead of feeling jealous of her?'

Chase drew her into his arms. 'You've forgiven her, Starre. That's the most important thing. You've forgiven her for being the person you wished you could be and being loved by the people you wanted to love you. Whatever happens, it's okay now.'

Starre seemed to wake up at his words. She headed to the car, Chase on her heels.

Please God, keep her safe. Let me see her again. Let me love her freely with your love. Help me show her the value of forgiveness so she can live with the same joy and freedom I have now I've forgiven Chase. Help her forgive her father!

***

Sky prayed as she wandered the hills, not sure which direction she should be heading. She searched for any sign of the campsite, but came up empty every time. How long till someone looked for her? Surely they wouldn't wait until it was dark?

But the sunlight was already fading and she was tired and hungry. She had missed lunch and probably dinner too. She strained her ears for the sound of voices, but everything was mixed up now with the buzzing in her head. At first she had thought every crow call had been someone coming for her. Birds whistling and calling shut out any other sound.

But then she saw a figure heading toward her. Finally. But she was too tired to move. She waited until he was close enough to recognise and her heart sank. Paul.

He rushed to her and he had a mobile phone to his ear. 'Yes, Dad, I found her. She seems okay …' He stopped and studied her, seeming breathless. 'Are you okay?'

She nodded as he spoke back into the phone.

'I'll bring her home, Dad. Speak to you soon.'

Then he just stood looking at her.

'I got lost.' Sky brushed at the tears, feeling dazed. 'Little Cloud bolted.'

'It's okay.' He sounded breathless. 'It happens.'

She stared up at him, and saw that he'd been afraid for her.

Then she remembered her horse and overcome by weariness, broke into helpless sobs.

'Sky,' he begged, 'don't cry.'

'But I lost Little Cloud.'

'It doesn't matter.'

She looked at him disbelievingly and he gave a not altogether controlled laugh. 'Come on, Sky! I thought we had lost *you*.'

She frowned in confusion. 'Me?'

'Yes. When you didn't come back I imagined all sorts of things.' He reached a gentle hand to her face and stroked her cheek. 'I've been doing some serious thinking. I don't know what I would have done if something happened to you. I couldn't have lived with myself.'

'What?'

He gave a lopsided smile. 'I know now that I completely misunderstood you. Now that I understand who you really are ...'

She reached a shaking hand to touch the fingers that rested gently on her cheek, unable to take her eyes from his face. His serious brown eyes were looking at her with such intensity she almost flinched under their scrutiny. Avoiding them, she studied his cleft chin and determined jaw, then stopped at his mouth. She saw the corners turn up as though he were about to smile.

'Want to see how they feel?' he asked quietly.

'What?' Her eyes flew to his.

'My lips.'

'Paul, I wasn't meaning ... I wasn't thinking ...'

'Maybe not, but I was.'

Her face flamed as his finger moved to her mouth. Gently he ran his finger along her lips. 'I've always wondered what it would be like to kiss you. Even when I was annoyed with you I had to admit I was attracted to you.'

'But you don't even like me.' Her voice cracked and she wished she could think straight and see through the cloud in her brain.

She heard Paul laugh deep in his throat. 'I tried very hard not to, but then I saw what everyone else was discerning enough to see in you and I couldn't help but fall for you too.'

Sky was confused. 'Paul.' Her voice was pleading. 'I don't understand.'

He nodded, a tender smile lighting his face. 'I know. I can't explain, though. Can I have permission to show you?'

Sky hesitated and in that moment he drew her into his arms and held her tight against his chest. Warmth filled her as she sank into the comfort of his arms. 'I have developed feelings for you,' he said, but with her ear against his chest, she wasn't sure she heard properly. She struggled out of his hold and stared up at him. He nodded his head in confirmation that she had indeed heard right.

'I have feelings for you,' he said again, this time his voice becoming husky, 'They're deep and strong and confusing. More than anything I want to kiss you, but I've never kissed anyone that way before.'

Suddenly she was back in that moment she had first seen him. Her heart was pounding and she couldn't think. She looked up at him. It was clear he was waiting, hoping. Mesmerised by the warmth in his melting brown eyes, she found herself moving toward him. 'Should I ... do you want me to?'

'Please.'

She gave a shaky smile, wondering at the way his confidence seemed to have left him. She was nervous but determined.

'I haven't either,' she whispered, just before their lips met briefly, gently.

'You haven't ever kissed anyone that way?' Paul's expression was incredulous as he broke away. His shock stung her.

'No.' Hurt welled up inside as she raised her chin. 'I've had boyfriends, but I'm not ... I don't throw myself at them like you seem to think I do.'

'I wasn't meaning—'

'You were! You haven't really changed your opinion of me, Paul Seton!'

Tears stung her eyes as she turned to run from him. She'd just given him a part of herself she'd wanted to keep for someone special who loved, respected, trusted her. She'd always decided she wouldn't kiss anybody until she was at least sixteen. And that wasn't for another two months. She'd just made a big mistake. Her head ached horribly. She had to get home.

'Sky,' he pleaded, coming after her, but she turned fiery dark eyes back to him.

'I don't run because I want to be followed, Paul! I'm not that type of girl either. So please leave me some dignity.'

He kept coming after her, and reached for her arm, but she wrenched it from him. 'I mean it, Paul!' She gritted her teeth, unable to help the tears that were now flowing freely. 'If you respected me you would let me go! If you really want to help me, show me the direction back to camp, then go and find Little Cloud and bring her home.'

Helplessly, Paul stopped in his tracks and pointed down the hill. 'Once you get to the bottom you'll see the creek. Turn left and follow it.'

Filled with a second wind, Sky ran without looking back.

She ran into camp, her eyes red from crying, her throat stinging from breathing so hard.

Kathina met her at the door of their cabin and threw her arms around her. 'It's okay, Sky. It's going to be okay.'

Sky shook her head. 'No, Kathina. I kissed him. He doesn't even love me and I kissed him!'

Kathina nodded. 'I know. He told me.'

What? How could he have? He was still out there looking for Little Cloud.

Kathina pointed to the mobile phone sitting on her suitcase. Sky frowned. Phones weren't allowed in camp.

'Where'd that come from?'

'It's Prince's. He was out looking for you and wanted me to keep in touch with him and Paul. Paul rang me. And he found Little Cloud.'

Her shoulders sagged with relief, but as she looked into Kathina's concerned eyes she remembered the way Paul had looked at her; the way he'd looked at Kathina first. 'I'm so sorry.' Helpless tears rolled down her cheeks. 'I should never have kissed him.'

She almost smiled. 'I don't have any claim on him. You don't need to apologise to me.' She patted the covers of Sky's bed. 'Just get some sleep. That's what you need right now.'

Sky started to protest, but once Kathina pushed her toward the bed she realised just how tired she was. Within minutes she was fast asleep.

***

Kathina waited until Blaze and Bonnie were by Sky's sleeping form before she headed out to wait for Paul. He'd made such a mess of everything. How could she feel so angry with him but sorry for him at the same time?

Of course he would be attracted to Sky; every teenage boy was. So why did he hurt her like that? How had he managed to get her to kiss him when kissing was something sacred to her? Sky had told her group last year that she'd never kissed a boy and didn't intend to unless he was someone she knew well and loved enough she thought she could marry him some day. And she'd said she'd wait until she was at least sixteen. What had Paul done to weaken that resolve?

By the time Paul arrived back with the horse, Kathina was more than angry. She was furious with him. He sauntered up, looking as strong and confident as ever. His warm brown eyes were studying her but she couldn't read his expression.

She stormed up to him. 'Well you got exactly what you

wanted, didn't you? You made her feel like all of us other girls in this world who struggle to accept God's love. You trampled her down. You made her lose her bubbly nature and carefree confidence. She feels inadequate and guilty.'

Paul stopped, twisting Little Cloud's tether around his hand. 'But I didn't mean to.'

'Shut up, Paul Seton. You've got no explaining to do to me. I know exactly what I saw you do and what a devastating effect it had on the closest friend I ever had. Now I might never get that friend back!'

Paul moved toward the fence where he tethered Little Cloud and began to check her over.

Kathina stood watching him, still seething. His silence infuriated her. 'Got nothing to say?'

Paul met the cold fury in her eyes and gave a sheepish grin. 'Well, I could say she's a good kisser, but I don't think that's what you want to hear. After all, *she* is clearly your best friend, not me.'

She couldn't believe her ears. She stepped forward and gave him a resounding slap across the cheek. Her hand stung with the force of it. Horrified, she put her hand across her mouth and gasped. She could see white finger marks surrounded by red on his cheek. Her eyes filled with tears. 'Oh, Paul, I'm so sorry.'

He wouldn't look at her. 'Let's talk in the morning.' He turned his face toward the horse and his voice was muffled.

'But Paul,'

'Please, Kathina.'

He didn't move, and so she slowly turned and walked away, trembling and unable to stop the tears streaming down her face. She'd just slapped the person she had thought she loved more than any other in the world; the one she refused to reveal her feelings to in case it made him uncomfortable. Well, he was certainly uncomfortable now.

Oh Lord, what have I done?

Chapter Twenty-Three

Sky opened her eyes, then blinked hard as she tried to focus. Her whole body hurt and her throat was sore. But there, sitting by her side were Bonnie and Blaze. Bonnie's hand was resting on her back, smoothing the covers someone had put over her.

'Mum. Dad.' She sat up, and immediately her parents' arms came about her. Her parents. Why hadn't she seen it before? Their eyes were alight with love as they held her tight. Blaze, so like Prince, but not quite as startlingly handsome, smiled down at her.

'I'm so glad you're okay,' he said, his voice husky with emotion. 'When you rang and told us about the incident with Joanna, I wanted to race here and be with you even though you said not to, but Bonnie reminded me you're a big girl now.'

'Big girl?' Sky chuckled at Bonnie. 'I could find that offensive, you know.'

Bonnie grinned back, blue eyes sparkling. 'Less offensive than me calling you a little girl, I'm sure.'

Sky grinned at them. 'So why are you here since I'm such a big girl?'

Blaze shook his head. 'Oh Sky, you are so loved. When I sent out the text saying you were missing, everyone wanted to come and look for you. Bonnie and I raced here as fast as we could. Prince and Rachel looked all afternoon. And your Aunty Starre is on her way here with Chase.'

Sky frowned. 'Chase, the circus guy? Why would he be coming?'

Blaze bit his lip. 'We're not sure. But Starre said he has something he wants to tell you. And she does too. I think it's something to do with when you were born.'

Bonnie reached for her hand. 'Everyone is waiting to see you. It's like the whole camp and our family are holding their breath, wanting to make sure you're okay. You've made your way into the hearts of so many people. You are a gift from God to every one of us.'

Sky's eyes filled with tears. 'But I just keep making a complete mess of everything, Mum.' She rubbed a hand across her mouth, remembering Paul's kiss. Was that how it was for Rachel when Prince seduced her? No, Rachel had known Prince from school and they'd developed a special friendship. What she felt for Paul went no deeper than a physical attraction. Jake's face filled her mind and her eyes slid shut.

'Mum, Dad, can you get Jake for me? I need to talk to him.'

She opened her eyes to see the look passing between her parents. Blaze stood and reached a hand to Bonnie to help her up. 'Of course. I'll see if we can find him.'

She heard his footsteps along the verandah and her heart pounded. She didn't even know what she wanted to say. She just needed to see him.

'Is it safe to come in?' His voice and eyes were laughing as he poked his head in the door. 'Don't want to break the rules now, do I?'

At the sight of his familiar smiling face and ginger hair, her eyes filled with tears. Annoyed, she tried to swipe them away. Immediately he stepped into the room and took the chair Blaze had been sitting on.

He turned the chair so he could face her directly and just watched her, waiting. She smoothed the wrinkles in the blanket on her bed, then finally lifted her eyes to meet his.

'Jake, I did something terrible. I gave away something that

… well, something I hoped to give to you someday.'

Jake's eyes widened and she saw the way his face drained of colour. Still, he waited for her to go on.

'I don't even know why I did it.' She was talking fast, now. 'He just, well, I was tired and I couldn't think and he wanted me to … so I did. I kissed him.' She was crying again, though she thought she'd have no tears left by now.

To her surprise, a look of relief passed through Jake's eyes and his shoulders relaxed. 'You kissed Paul?'

She nodded, the tears coming faster, now. 'I knew the mistakes my dad had made, about how I was a … well, a mistake. I decided I would never even kiss a guy until I was sixteen and only if I knew he was the one I wanted to marry. I didn't want to give away any part of me to the wrong person.'

Jake had reached over and wiped her tears with his fingers. 'Not even a kiss?'

She nodded, gazing at him, willing him to understand. He learned forward and cupped her face in his hands. He came closer until she could see nothing but his eyes and the sincerity there.

'Listen to me, Sky Clements. You're not a mistake. I don't even think your father believes that. And if you don't want to kiss until you're sure, that's fine with me. I respect your principles. But don't hold against yourself something that even God doesn't hold against you.'

Sky took a shaky breath. 'You're not upset?'

Jake chuckled as he let his hands fall from her face. 'Upset? What, that in a roundabout way you just told me you want to marry me someday? That you feel so committed to me you were compelled to confess you kissed someone else? That you've just told me you don't have feelings for the good looking Paul Seton after all? Which bit should upset me the most?'

His eyes were twinkling at her and she couldn't help letting a giggle escape. 'Well, when you put it like that.' She bit her lip.

'I've never had a relationship with a close friend before.'

He smiled. 'I've never had a girlfriend before, full stop.'

She grinned. 'But you've had me on your list of potential wives just the same.'

'Yes. My one person list, that is.'

She threw her arms around his neck and he pulled her close.

'I love you, Sky Clements,' he whispered into her hair, 'and I don't want to get this wrong, so let's pray.'

Sky nodded, then listened as his deep voice rumbled in her ear. His prayer, as always, was heartfelt and meaningful.

'Guide us, Lord,' he prayed. 'May this relationship be between you and me and Sky. Give us patience, understanding, self-control, and most of all, the deepest kind of love there is— your love. May we always be able to forgive one another when needed, communicate openly and honestly, and always bring glory to you. Amen.'

Sky echoed his amen then pulled back and smiled the way she hadn't felt like for several days; a beautiful, full smile that expressed the joy in her heart. 'I love you, Jake. Please come and visit me when camp is over.'

He took her hand. 'I will. Your parents won't be able to keep me away.'

'My parents,' she repeated softly. 'Blaze and Bonnie Clements. They're the best parents I could ever have wished for.'

'That's what I always thought,' he agreed, then pulled her into his arms for another hug.

***

Kathina watched as Sky emerged from the cabin, Jake by her side. She'd always thought it would happen someday. The friendship between Sky and Jake was deep and special, with God at the centre. Jake's obvious admiration for Sky and her respect for his spiritual maturity had made her suspect God had more than friendship for the two of them. It seemed she was right. But what about Paul? This would surely hurt him. As if she hadn't put him through enough last night.

'Kathina?'

She started at the sound of Paul's voice and knew he'd seen the way Sky and Jake held hands as they came from the cabin, gazing into one another's eyes.

'I'm sorry, Paul,' she tried to say, but her voice didn't come out properly.

'I deserved it.' He shrugged and she knew he was trying to hide what he really felt. 'I never thought you would do it, but I was asking for it.'

'No, I'm not talking about hitting you.' Kathina turned to him, letting him see the tears in her eyes. 'I'm sorry about that.' She nodded in the direction Jake and Sky had now gone.

'Why?' His brows met in confusion. 'What's that got to do with you?'

She swallowed hard. 'Nothing, really. I just know it's got to be hard for you. I'm sorry she's chosen Jake when you have feelings for her.'

Paul stared at her as though unable to believe what he was hearing. 'You have got to be the most unselfish, understanding person I have met in my life.'

Her eyes darted to his.

'It's true.' His eyes were wide with wonder. 'You completely ignore the fact that I've used you, overlooked you, hurt you, driven you to slap me—'

She opened her mouth to correct him, but he held out a hand to stop her. 'No, it's true. You would never hit anyone unless they were disrespecting and severely hurting someone you love. You didn't slap me for yourself. You slapped me for Sky.'

Kathina took a deep breath. Maybe that was true, but not completely. She was sure some of her own hurt and disappointment that Paul would never want to kiss her that way had played a part in her reaction.

'You might never respect me again, but I have to tell you this,' Paul said. She raised her eyes to his, waiting.

'I don't love Sky. Not that way. Maybe the teenage hormone part of me thought it would be exciting to kiss someone as outwardly beautiful as Sky. And maybe I have more respect for her than I used to have, but what I did yesterday was unacceptable. I was using her to satisfy my own curiosity and desire, and betraying you in the process.'

'Betraying me?' She let out half a chuckle. 'You owe me nothing, Paul.'

He just smiled at her, his serious brown eyes looking deep into hers. Then she saw it. The red streaks across his cheek. The place she had slapped him. Unable to help herself, she reached her hand and gently touched the place, pain making it hard to breathe.

'It's okay.' His voice was deep and soft. 'It was the most loving thing anyone has ever done to me. I've needed someone to slap some sense into me for a long time.'

With a half laugh, half cry, she shook her head, but he had reached to place his hand over hers across his cheek.

'It's true. You love me, don't you? You care so much you would give up your own feelings, your own desires to see me happy.'

'Paul, I'm not like the other girls. I'm not slim and beautiful and confident.'

Paul quirked an eyebrow. 'All the things I obviously respect and value in a girl.'

He was being sarcastic, but he had made his point. He had been physically attracted to Sky but it was clear he hadn't respected her. Kathina had always known he was the type of person to look deeper; to want more. Yet he'd disappointed her. The mature, Godly young man had shown he had another side this week and she didn't feel like she could trust him right now.

She removed his hand from the top of hers.

'Paul, it's been a big week. We're all exhausted and so much has happened. Let's talk more when we get home, when life gets back to normal.'

He didn't argue, but his brown eyes held hers with something she knew was a promise.

***

Sky stopped short as she was met by the cheers of campers. And then she was swarmed upon as everyone moved to hug her at once. Paul stood to the side and her eyes met his. If only she'd never fallen for him. She'd made a mess of everything. She didn't deserve all this love.

'Forgiven, remember,' a voice said in her ear and she turned to smile at Jake. She tightened her fingers around his. Then she saw Blaze's eyes widen as he quirked an eyebrow at her. She tried not to giggle. After last year's camp she had told her parents about her friend, Jake. She'd also told them she cared for him and respected him but that no romantic feelings were involved.

'It's better if friendship comes first, anyway,' Bonnie had told her, but Sky had disagreed. She was determined she would fall deeply and madly in love with the man of her dreams. It would be love at first sight and there would be no looking back.

How wrong she'd been.

'Mum, Dad, I want you to meet Jake.'

Jake stepped forward to shake Blaze's hand. 'Mr Clements,' he gave a nod to Bonnie, 'Mrs Clements. Nice to meet you.'

Blaze grinned. 'So, can we expect to see a bit of you in the future?' He nodded pointedly toward their entwined hands.

'I'm hoping so,' Jake admitted, his expression open and sincere.

Blaze chuckled. 'I like you already. You're not the type Sky usually falls for though; the smooth-faced, mysterious type.'

'Dad!'

151

Blaze grinned at Sky's embarrassment. 'What? You told me yourself he's the more rugged type with deep laugh lines around his mouth and mature, honest eyes you can trust.'

Jake was grinning. 'She said that?'

Sky buried her face in her hand while Blaze shrugged. 'Something along those lines.'

Jake waited until Sky looked at her again. 'So you've loved me for a while, even if you didn't admit it.'

Sky wished the warmth would leave her cheeks as she smiled at him and shrugged. 'Must have.'

Chapter Twenty-Four

Starre's grip tightened on the steering wheel as they drove through the gate and into the camp centre. Chase reached across and squeezed her shoulder. She smiled at him. 'You ready for this?'

He straightened his good leg then tightened the brace on his other. 'Ready as I'll ever be. Where did Blaze say to meet them?'

'In the meeting room. Most of the campers are in the hall, so he said everyone else would be in the meeting room behind the kitchen.'

Chase strained her eyes. 'I wonder which way the kitchen is.'

Starre chuckled as she pointed. 'I'm sure that group of people will direct us.'

Chase looked too and laughed. 'That's them, isn't it? Couldn't even wait until we got here.'

Starre nodded. 'They're like that. Blaze is, anyway. It's like he thinks it's his duty to keep an eye on us all and keep looking out for us as a family.' Her voice softened. 'I didn't make it easy for him, but he never gave up on me. Just like God didn't.'

'I didn't either.'

His voice was so soft she wondered if she imagined his words. But when she glanced at him, his eyes were watching her tenderly. She took a deep breath and pulled into the car park. 'Let's do this, Chase. Together.'

He nodded and they both opened their doors at the same time. Starre saw Prince first and she laughed as she threw her arms around him. 'Well, you didn't let age take your looks, did you?'

Prince laughed as he ruffled her hair. 'You don't look too bad yourself.'

'So you're going to be working here at the camp centre?'

Prince nodded. 'Yes. A whole lot closer to Blaze and Bonnie. And Sky.'

She looked up to see that Blaze himself was waiting beside Prince, his dark eyes filled with joy. 'You haven't aged too badly either,' she teased him, before he closed the distance between them and drew her into a brotherly hug.

She was drawn from one set of arms to another, but it was Sky she was waiting to see. She glanced around until her eyes rested on a girl who looked so like herself her breath stuck in her throat. Despite her smile, she looked overwhelmed. Dark waves of hair flowed down around her shoulders and her perfectly smooth skin and dazzling smile took Starre's breath away. Her niece. Sky.

She looked around for Chase. He was now talking to Prince, but he stopped when his eyes met hers. Reaching a hand to him, she drew him over to where Sky stood.

'Sky, I want you to meet Chase, the man who cared for you when you were a newborn. Who protected you from his father's manipulative plans for you and from your mother's neglect. The man who could only give you up when he knew there were others who loved you so deeply they would never abandon you.'

Sky was looking up, studying Chase's scarred face, but there was no horror in her expression. Only awe. Starre breathed a sigh of relief. She'd had no idea how Sky would react to his appearance.

Chase was gazing at her, his eyes glistening. 'Sky, you're so loved, but you just can't see it.'

Sky swallowed hard. 'I see it,' she whispered. Then she threw her arms around Chase and held him tightly. He raised his eyes heavenward and Starre knew he was thanking God for Sky and the opportunity to see her again.

Sky turned to Blaze and gave him an equally fierce hug. Then she searched the group until her eyes rested on Prince. With a cry, she ran to him and held him as though she would never let go.

Starre swallowed the lump in her throat. How could she have held herself aloof from this girl? From her whole family? She had denied herself so much joy and love.

The chatter as they all entered the meeting room was overwhelming. Prince, Blaze and Chase were deep in conversation and Starre knew they were talking about the past; working it all through and beginning to understand what had really happened.

Then Rachel was by her side. 'So good to see you, Starre.' Rachel's warm brown eyes met hers in genuine joy. Her voice was just as musical as she had remembered it from high school. 'It's been so long but life just gets so busy. I guess looking after rescue animals is a twenty-four hour job. No creature realises it's the weekend so holds off getting injured until Monday.'

Starre chuckled, amused. 'No. They don't really stick to a schedule. A bit like your psychology patients, I guess.'

Rachel smiled. 'Yes.' She tilted her head to the side. 'There's something I've always wondered. Is there a way you can chase up animals? I mean, I know dogs and cats are microchipped, but is there a way you can trace horses?'

Starre hesitated. 'Why?'

Rachel let out a heartfelt sigh. 'Prince has always regretted selling Regal Zion. I suggested he try to find him, but he said he doesn't know where to begin.' Sadness filled her eyes. 'He also says he doesn't deserve to have him back. He sold him on a whim. He was scared Regal would get tetanus like Peter Pan. And he didn't want to think about the circus anymore.'

Starre's heart skipped a beat. She had only recently forgiven Prince for selling Regal Zion. Now she understood why he'd done it. Should she tell Rachel that Regal Zion belonged to Chase; that he now waited in the Animal Rescue yards and she was caring for him?

Instead, she smiled at Rachel. 'There are ways. Leave it with me.'

'Thank you!' Rachel seemed breathless with gratitude. 'I've been praying about it. I know it would be a miracle, but I know how much it would mean to him.'

Starre nodded, feeling trapped. Regal Zion was a coveted horse. She wanted him. Prince wanted him. Blaze wanted him, or rather, a rescue horse like him, for Sky. But he belonged to Chase.

God, give us wisdom. Help Chase know what to do.

***

Sky looked around, searching for her siblings. Bonnie said she'd met Seton and Blythe when she was four and they were babies, but she couldn't remember. She approached Prince. 'Where is everyone else?'

Prince smiled. 'The kids are outside. I couldn't drag them away from the horses.'

Sky's heart sank. They didn't want to meet her? But Prince had taken her arm. 'I'll take you. They made me promise I'd take you out there once all the "huggie stuff" as they call it, settled down.'

Sky grinned. 'Nothing wrong with huggie stuff!'

'That's what I tried to tell them. Maybe you'll have better luck.'

Sky saw her youngest sibling first. Ten year old Philippa was standing on the back of a cantering horse. She was nimble and lithe and her dark hair flowed out behind her. Sky felt as though she were looking at a younger version of herself.

'She's amazing!' She reached the fence and leaned against it, unable to take her eyes from the girl. A movement caught her attention and she turned to see two dark haired teens sitting on the fence rail to her left. She hadn't noticed them, she was so caught up in watching Philippa.

Prince moved toward them. 'Seton, Blythe, meet Sky.'

The two grinned matching grins at exactly the same moment

as they jumped from the rail and landed nimbly on the ground.

'Good to meet ya, finally,' Seton said, his dark eyes twinkling at her in a friendly manner, 'but couldn't you have been a boy?'

'Seton!' Blythe's eyes widened in horror as she stared at her brother. 'Don't start. You've only just met her!'

She then turned laughing eyes much like her twin's to Sky. 'He asks me that same question all the time. As if we need another boy like him around here causing trouble.'

Seton shook his mop of curly black hair. 'I don't cause trouble. I just liven the place up a bit.' He put his arm around his twin's neck, then pulled her into a headlock. 'Isn't that right, Blythe?' He messed her hair with his free hand. 'Isn't that what you meant to say?'

'Dad, help me!' Blythe yelled, but she didn't need to. With a laugh, Sky leaped at him and wrestled him until he let Blythe go.

'Hey, not fair!' He shook his tousled head. 'I told you we need another boy around here.'

Blythe gave him a triumphant look. 'Thought you said you were strong enough to take us all on. You reckoned you were worth ten of us girls.'

Seton screwed up his face. 'No comment.'

'Ha! Only because you have no response. I win again.' She let out a scream as Seton ran at her and Sky watched them, unable to help laughing. She had only just met them and she loved them already. If only she could have grown up with them and been a part of this amazing family.

She stopped mid-thought as Bonnie appeared at her side. She was laughing at them with abandon and joy shining from her brilliant blue eyes. No, not even this family could replace Bonnie and Blaze. They were amazing parents who loved her completely. How could she ever want more?

'So this is Philippa?' Sky asked as the girl leapt from the back of the horse and made her way over. Her body seemed to float and each movement flowed as though she were dancing.

'Watching her takes me back in time,' Bonnie said in Sky's ear. 'I remember a whole family who moved like her. The school stopped and stared at them when they first arrived.'

'Did Uncle Blaze used to walk like that too?'

Bonnie smiled. 'When he was performing, yes. But with Prince and Starre it came naturally all the time. Philippa's the same.'

Sky felt as though she were catching a glimpse into the lives of the performing circus family all those years ago. Blaze had told her many stories about his younger siblings—the triplets and twins—who'd performed in the circus with him as children. She loved to hear the stories but she had never imagined what it had been like until now. If they were like Philippa, they were born to be stars. She couldn't keep her eyes off her.

'I'm Philippa,' the girl said with a cheeky grin much like the twins'.

'Lover of horses,' Sky agreed with a smile. 'Yes, your name suits you perfectly.'

'Thanks,' she said looking shy all of a sudden. Then her eyes brightened. 'Want to meet Abel Tasman?'

A puzzled look flashed through Sky's eyes, and Seton let out a hoot of laughter. 'It's her horse, Sky. Abel is her horse.'

Philippa scowled in Seton's direction. 'She knew that.'

Sky hadn't, but she didn't want to be caught in the middle of an argument, so she pulled Philippa's arm. 'Come on, I need to meet him!'

Philippa cast a triumphant look in Seton's direction and led the way.

'He's amazing.'

Sky had to agree as she stroked the horse's nose. 'He has the most beautiful colouring I've seen in a horse.'

Philippa looked pleased but Seton was there. 'Regal Zion was more amazing than him.'

Philippa opened her mouth, clearly about to object but Seton didn't let her get a word in. 'Regal Zion was Dad's horse in the circus. Have you seen pictures of him?'

'Not that I remember,' Sky admitted. 'I'd like to, though.'

Seton looked at Prince. 'Dad, have you still got those pictures on your phone?'

Prince nodded and pulled his mobile phone from his pocket. 'I scanned all the old pictures.' He moved toward Sky, swiping his thumb across the screen and smiling as he stopped and moved closer so Sky could see the pictures. He began to swipe through, and Sky stood, transfixed.

There were pictures of the whole family, including Blaze, riding their horses around the ring. Victorian Dream, one of the triplets' horses, was the largest, but none of the horses were quite like Regal Zion.

Sky studied the photo of young Prince Clements on his horse. She knew she'd never seen a more beautiful creature than that horse in her life. His sleek lines and unique colouring made him appear surreal. He looked straight at the camera as though he knew what a magnificent creature he was and there was a sparkle in his eye. 'He looks almost human.'

'That's because he was treated as human,' Prince said with a laugh. 'He thought he was. He had more personality than a lot of humans I've known.'

Prince moved his face closer to the phone and Sky saw the shadow that crossed his eyes as she gazed at it. 'I've always wondered what happened to Regal Zion.' His voice had turned soft. 'Some days I miss him so much it hurts. I know he's just an animal, but to me he was a friend and partner. We worked together in that ring every day and we understood each other.'

'What happened to him?'

Prince shrugged. 'I sold him in a hurry. You know, kind of as a reaction to everything that was going on. I didn't let myself think about it. I listed him in *Equizine*, a horse magazine, and he was snapped up really fast. I only needed a few thousand for the motorbike. Regal Zion was worth way more than the five thousand I got for him.'

'Do you know who bought him?'

Prince shook his head sadly. 'At the time I didn't want to know. If I was going to give him up I needed to break free of him completely. Otherwise I knew I'd change my mind.'

'So you could never buy him back?'

Prince gave a dry laugh. 'Not unless his new owner is as stupid as I was. There's no way someone in their right mind would sell him for the amount I sold him for.'

'But what about all those dressage horses you sold?'

Prince hesitated for a moment, then he shrugged. 'We're giving that money to this camp centre. We prayed about it and felt that was what we were meant to do. They couldn't have set up their trail riding if we hadn't helped out.'

Sky's heart felt heavy as she listened to Prince. His face was filled with regret and she wished she could do something. *Lord, if there is any way he can get Regal Zion back, please provide the way!*

***

Starre sighed as her phone rang. She looked apologetically at Blaze. 'Sorry, it's my boss. I'd better get this.'

Blaze nodded with a smile. 'Go ahead. You're fine.'

She moved to the window. 'Hey Bruce. Is Regal Zion all right?' She kept her voice quiet, not wanting Blaze to hear.

'Yeah, he's great. But listen, I've got some news.' Bruce sounded excited. 'There's a television company wanting to support Animal Rescue and they want to do a documentary on our centre.'

Starre couldn't help laughing. 'Hey, that's great. The more people know about us, the better.'

'Yeah, but listen, Starre, they came to look around and I told them Regal Zion's story. Now they want to take it further.'

'Further? What do you mean?'

'They want to do a story on the rescue centre, but focus on Regal Zion.' He cleared his throat. 'And they suggested getting footage of him being reunited with your brother. You know, a feel-good story, showing just how important what we do really is.'

Starre's jaw dropped. She didn't know what to think or feel.

Is this how you're directing me, God? I need to tell Prince about Regal Zion, don't I?

'Starre?'

'Sorry Bruce. Thinking.'

'I know. It's a big thing to ask.'

Yes, he was right about that. She took a deep breath. 'Bruce, I'll get back to you, okay?'

'Thanks Starre. But think how much it will mean for Animal Rescue.'

And Prince. And Regal Zion. But what about Chase? I need to talk to him. 'I know Bruce. I'll pray about it.'

The words had slipped out before she could stop them. She hadn't told Bruce about her newfound faith. She bit her lip, wondering what his response would be.

'Okay, but I think God likes a feel good story, too. Maybe this is his way of helping the animals you believe he created.'

Starre laughed. 'How do you know I believe he made animals?'

Bruce grunted. 'You'd be stupid not to. No creature so complex could be an act of chance.'

'You believe too?' Starre couldn't help laughing at the wonder of it. She had never asked Bruce what he believed.

'Not in all that Jesus stuff, but I believe there is a God.'

Starre smiled. Once she told him the full story of Regal Zion and the forgiveness she had found, he might just believe in Jesus, too. 'I'll be in touch soon, Bruce.'

'Thanks Starre. You're a star.'

She chuckled and ended the call, unsure if he had meant to be funny or not. Then she turned to find Chase. They needed to talk.

Chase agreed Prince needed to be told about Regal Zion. 'But you'd better protect me if he comes at me.' He grinned at Starre. 'I can't run like I used to.'

'Oh Chase.' Starre put her arms around his neck. 'How could he be angry with you?'

His grey eyes twinkled at her. 'You were, remember?'

That stopped her. 'Oh. But not about that.'

'You sure? 'Cause it sure looked to me like your eyes were flashing fire that day you came in before you even knew who I was.'

She giggled. 'Flashing fire?'

'Shooting sparks. Flaming fury.'

She playfully shoved his shoulder. 'Flaming affection, you mean.'

His brows rose. 'Before you even recognised me? Is it a habit of yours; *flaming affection* for perfect strangers?'

She bit her lip. 'Um, no, okay, maybe I was a bit upset. But I didn't know the full story. If we just slowly tell the full story, Prince will be fine. He'll be overjoyed, even. How could he not be?'

Chase put his arm around her and drew her closer, speaking into her ear. 'Are *you* overjoyed?'

Her eyes connected with his and her breathing became unsteady. 'I am, actually.' She tried to pull herself together. She couldn't fall for him again. Forgiveness was about not holding something against someone; it didn't require deliberately putting yourself in the path of more hurt.

No, that's grace.

Grace. Like God had extended to her. More than forgiveness; not giving her what she deserved, but grace; giving her the love, joy and blessings she didn't deserve.

Before she could settle her heart, Chase had stepped back.

'So do we call a family meeting or what?'

***

Sky couldn't help feeling nervous as she looked around the circle of her family. Everyone was seated, their eyes on Starre and Chase. She wished Jake were by her side, but he and Marion and Charles had camp duties to perform. The camp couldn't stop just because her life was so overwhelming right now. Kathina was taking over her role for the remainder of the camp.

Chase looked so serious. Nervous even. She wondered how he'd been injured. The scars down his cheek marred what was obviously a handsome face and his left knee was covered by a sophisticated-looking brace.

Chase leaned forward. 'Starre had a call from the Animal Rescue centre this morning. It could change a lot of things.' He looked at Starre, and she nodded. Sky smiled. Was a romance blooming there? Had her mother's final words sorted things out between them?

'So I thought I'd tell you our story all at once. I know I told some of you about how Starre and I met up again when she was called to rescue one of my animals.' He licked his lips. 'It was my horse. I'd been injured on duty, rescuing some kids.' His eyes went to Sky. 'I wanted to make up for not being able to look after you; for all the injustice in the world.'

Sky was aware all eyes had turned to her, but she couldn't tear her gaze away from the genuine tenderness in Chase's expression.

'I also wanted to make up for the way I hurt Starre. Dad had a strong hold over me, one I should never have let him have. When he told me to seduce Starre so you guys would stay in the circus I had no problems with that. But when, just two days later, he found out Carrie was pregnant with Prince's baby and wanted to keep the baby, he made me change my story. I told everyone that Carrie's baby was mine, just like he told me to.'

Sky heard the intakes of breath around her and felt sorry for

163

Chase. He looked nervous as he looked down at his feet. But she was spellbound. She wanted to understand.

Starre put a hand on his arm and Chase seemed to gain courage to continue the story. 'When Carrie's alcohol problem stopped her being able to care for Sky, I took over. But then Marcos kidnapped Starre, hoping she would see that Sky was Prince's and convince your family to return to the circus. He never counted on Blaze being so protective and contacting Family Services to take on Sky.'

Sky's eyes flew to Blaze. Being the eldest of the Clements siblings, he'd always had a father's heart. He called his brothers and sisters every week and kept a track of them. Being the first Christian in the family had also given him a feeling of responsibility and genuine love for them all. She was privileged to have had him as her father all these years.

'I hated Chase.' Starre's voice was filled with regret as she continued the story. 'I attacked him that day. I was jealous of the way I could see he loved Sky and put her needs before mine. And I never told anyone what happened, but I shut my heart off to love. I've lived with a barrier around my heart until only a few weeks ago. I got a call out. A horse stuck in barbed wire.'

Starre's eyes shot to Prince, then away again.

Chase, however looked directly at him. 'It was my horse. One I bought years ago when my dad tried to buy it. It was the final straw for me. I bought the horse and left the circus to become a cop. I thought I would sell it back to the real owner if he wanted him back some day.'

Sky glanced around the room. No one moved. The group were listening, waiting. Starre wiped her hands down her shorts and she and Chase looked at one another. It was as though both held their breaths.

'It was Regal Zion. I bought Regal Zion before Dad could.'

The words came out of Chase's mouth so quickly that

everyone took a moment to register them.

Prince came to his feet. 'But I was told it was a guy with a special needs child.'

Chase nodded. 'That was the story my dad made up. He wanted Regal Zion so badly. He paid some guys to get him on his behalf. But I got in first.'

Prince paled. 'So you're telling me you have Regal Zion?'

Chase and Starre nodded at once. 'He's at the rescue centre.'

Prince fell back into his chair, and Rachel's arm came around him. She had tears rolling down her cheeks. Sky could hardly believe what she was hearing. Sometimes God arranged answers to prayer before you even prayed.

Starre was speaking again and Sky forced herself to focus. 'So Bruce asked if we can all be involved in the documentary. It will be our story; Regal Zion's story. We'll be paid for it.'

Everyone was looking at one another. Then Blaze stood. 'We'll have to contact Misty, Storm and Beauty. We can't do this without their permission.'

Prince nodded. 'Fame isn't all it's cracked up to be. I want to be involved in the actual production. I have training in media so maybe they'll let me work for them. I want to make sure we're all happy with how it's done. We want a true representation. And we want to make sure everyone is happy for the story to be out there.'

Everyone nodded and Blaze bowed his head. 'Let's pray and ask God for wisdom and guidance.'

As he prayed, Sky couldn't help her smile. God was doing something special, something beyond all she could have dreamed. She was part of an amazing family and they were all so loved by God.

Chapter Twenty-Five

Camp was a bustle of activity as rooms were packed up and amenities cleaned. Alexa chatted comfortably as she helped Sky pull down the posters from the walls of the cabin.

'Prince and Rachel offered to adopt Joanna and me,' she told Kathina and Sky. 'But I was too scared. After the way my dad hurt me I thought no one could really want me. I thought they were just putting on an act, being nice and all. I started being really difficult, saying I would kill myself and everything, but they didn't take back the offer.'

'So did you accept?' Kathina asked.

Alexa glanced at her, then concentrated hard on the poster of the horse in front of her. 'No. I wanted to, but I knew if I was adopted, well, I could never ...'

Sky and Kathina waited. Finally, Alexa looked directly at Kathina. 'It doesn't matter now. He's yours anyway. And after the way he treated Sky, I just, well ...'

Understanding dawned. 'You couldn't be Paul's girlfriend if you were his adopted sister?'

Alexa nodded.

Kathina sighed deeply. 'Lexi, he's not mine. To tell you the truth, I feel a bit like you. After the way he treated Sky this week ...'

It was there that Sky cut in. 'Now just hold it there, you two! I've forgiven Paul, so don't hold against him what even I don't. He's a decent guy. He just got muddled up like we all do sometimes.'

Kathina looked as though she hadn't heard. She was studying the curtains she'd adjusted to fit the window at the beginning of the week. 'Do you think we should leave these here?'

Sky laughed and came to stand between her and the curtains. 'Kathina, are you hearing what I'm saying?'

She bit her lip. 'I hear you.'

'Lexi?'

Lexi grinned. 'Yeah, yeah.'

'No, I'm serious. Forgiveness, remember? Love of a Heavenly Father who gave everything for us. That's what this whole week has been about. Let's not just believe it in our heads, let's live it!'

Lexi and Kathina were grinning at each other.

'What?'

Kathina shrugged. 'You're so passionate. How could we dare go against you?'

They continued cleaning. Sky had just zipped up her suitcase when Alexa put a photo on the lid in front of her. 'That's my parents. Since you asked when we first arrived.'

Sky looked down at the picture, then up to her. 'Your father looks so happy there.'

She nodded. 'That was before Mum died. Before he started drinking.' She swallowed hard. 'I'm going to go and visit him in jail. Tell him I forgive him. Then I'm going to let Prince and Rachel adopt me.'

Sky grinned from ear to ear. 'You know what?' She stood to give Alexa a hug. 'You've been nowhere near as much trouble as I was expecting.'

Alexa laughed out loud, her expression teasing. 'Really? Camp's not over yet, Sky Clements. I could show you just how much trouble I can really be.'

Prince and Blaze came into the cabin to help the girls take out their suitcases.

'These camps are invaluable,' Blaze was saying to Prince. 'Sky came back a changed girl after her first one.' He hesitated. 'Do all your children believe?'

Prince nodded. 'My own do, yes.'

'Your foster child does too,' a voice said quietly, and both looked to where Alexa had come to her foster father's side. 'I believe now.'

A cry of joy came from Prince as he drew Alexa to his side then raised his eyes heavenward. 'Thank you, God, for bringing another child home.'

Alexa grinned sheepishly at Kathina and Sky, clearly embarrassed but pleased by Prince's reaction.

Blaze's face lit into a smile too and Sky raced to his side to give him a hug. Alexa stepped back from Prince, suddenly looking uncertain. 'And Dad, I'd like to be adopted if that offer is still there.'

Prince seemed unable to speak. He simply drew Alexa closer into his arms and held her tight. Finally he pulled back, smiling at her. 'Let's go and tell your new mother, shall we?'

Sky watched on, surprised it didn't hurt. Instead, it brought her a joy she could never have imagined. Forgiveness truly was a miracle that had set her free; free to love and be loved.

Goodbyes were always the hardest thing about camps. This one was the hardest of them all. So much had happened that Sky doubted she would be able to settle into normal life ever again. It was easy enough to leave Paul, Alexa and her father; she would see them all again soon. It wasn't so easy to say goodbye to Kathina. Sky knew she was still troubled and hurt by Paul and it bothered her.

She helped the girl put her bag into the back of her parents' car. 'I hope and pray you can sort it all out before Paul moves here to the camp centre.'

Kathina shook her head. 'Maybe we can't sort it out. Maybe that's why God chose to bring him here, so I don't have to see him every day. I'm sure going to miss the old Paul, though.'

Sky held her friend tight. 'Forgiveness, remember,' she

whispered. 'The old Paul is still there.'

She watched as Kathina and Harrison left in their parents' car.

Her final goodbye was the hardest of all. Jake stood before her, his eyes speaking when he couldn't.

'Come and see me soon?' she whispered. She would still be able to visit him, just like she could visit Prince, but she would miss seeing Jake every day, having his support and comforting presence.

He simply nodded before drawing her into an embrace. She felt herself responding to him in every way and wished she could stay in his strong arms. She'd never imagined she could feel so much for someone. This was more than infatuation. This went far deeper than anything she'd ever known. She wanted to tell him she loved him, but no words came out.

'Your parents are waiting,' he said softly into her hair and joy filled her being. Blaze and Bonnie. Her parents. Tears rimmed her eyes and she managed a husky goodbye before she pulled back from Jake and went to join them in the car.

They were only just out the gate when Sky leaned forward in her seat. 'Mum? Dad? Am I too old to be adopted now? Is it too late?'

Her heart pounded, almost fearing the answer.

She saw the way her parents' eyes met before they both turned back to her. The car swerved and Sky laughed.

Bonnie put a hand on Blaze's arm. 'Maybe we should pull over.'

Blaze gave a sheepish grin and did. Then they both turned to face her in their seats.

Blaze spoke first. 'Never too late. It would bring us both the greatest joy.'

Bonnie was looking at her as though she didn't dare hope. She reached a hand to touch Sky. 'What made you decide?'

She sighed. 'I didn't want you to adopt me because ... well, I thought if my own father didn't want me I didn't deserve a real family.'

Both Blaze and Bonnie let out a gasp, and Blaze's hand

tightened on hers. 'Oh, Sky, you've been a joy and delight to us, the greatest gift God could have given us. When we found out we couldn't have our own children, we were okay. It didn't hurt as much because we had you.'

Sky's eyes widened. 'You can't have children?'

Bonnie nodded. 'The doctors aren't sure whether it's a result of Blaze having had tetanus, or a result of my injuries when I went into the burning stables to rescue Regal Zion—'

That was Regal Zion? Sky had heard the story of Bonnie saving one of the Clements' horses but she'd never realised it was her father's horse she'd been rescuing.

'But I had always thought, I always presumed …' She struggled to continue. 'I thought that maybe you didn't have other children because of me. Because I was so much work, especially when I went through that stage when I was so angry with Prince. And I wanted to do gymnastics and swimming and, well, everything. I thought you just didn't have time for your own children. I felt bad, but Prince didn't seem to want me and I didn't know where else to go.'

Bonnie let out a cry and threw open her door. Sky couldn't open her own door fast enough. She leapt from the car and into Bonnie's waiting arms.

'Oh, my Sky, how could you have thought that? I put everything into you because you're all I have. I wanted to do all those things for you and I thought it would make you love us more, maybe make you want to be ours for always.'

Blaze had come to join them now and he held them both. He swallowed hard, as though trying to hold back his own emotion.

Sky bit her lip. 'I haven't asked Prince what he thinks. Do you think he'll be okay with it?'

'I'm sure he will be.' Blaze looked to Bonnie. 'I was talking to him about it just this morning. He admitted one of the reasons he didn't try to take you back earlier was that he couldn't bring himself to take you from us. He knows we can't have our own children. He also admitted he's always felt a bit like it's his fault.'

Bonnie's eyes widened. 'What?'

Blaze shrugged. 'Well, it was his horse you went into the stables to save. And you went to all that effort and then he sold Regal Zion.'

Bonnie shook her head, then faced Sky. 'One of my greatest fears has been that Prince would take you back. I encouraged him to leave you with us; to let you be settled. I had no idea of the heartache it caused you. My fear and selfishness hurt you and I'm so sorry. I just couldn't let you go; couldn't leave you in God's hands the way I should have.'

Sky looked into Bonnie's brilliant blue eyes, sparkling with unshed tears. Her mother. She was burned but beautiful. A burning stable couldn't steal true beauty, just like Joanna scarring her wouldn't have stolen the joy and inner beauty that came from God.

Blaze brought her attention back. 'Sky, I'd love you to be ours. Officially ours. Prince signed the papers years ago. I'm not sure if we need them updated.'

Sky smiled. 'I always have been yours, really. But yes, let's do it. Let's sign the adoption papers. And Uncle Blaze?' She raised her eyes to his. 'Can I call you Dad?'

He gave a part cough and cleared his throat as his eyes shone. 'I'd love you to.' He cleared his throat again and smiled wide. 'Right now I think I have a bit of an understanding of what God feels when one of his children finally comes home and accept him as their Heavenly Father.'

Chapter Twenty-Six

Starre helped Chase load Regal Zion onto the horse float. It was a long way to Camp Oaken, but the horse was healed enough that he would handle the journey. In fact, he looked magnificent.

The television presenters had spoken to each of the family members and were ready for the reunion of Regal Zion and Prince. They were impressed with Prince's qualifications and agreed to have him work for them throughout the production.

Bruce was delighted. 'Our centre will be known all around the country. Animal Rescue doesn't get near enough publicity or promotion, so this is an amazing opportunity.'

Starre glanced at Chase. He was listening quietly and his subdued manner bothered her. Courtney had left him for good, he was no longer able to be in the job he loved, and he was now giving up his horse. She wished she knew what would cheer him up.

God, please show him what you have for him. Give him a job he can love. Fulfil his deepest desires.

Chase's voice interrupted her prayer. 'Well, let's get on the road.' He gave her a sideways look. 'Thanks for inviting me.'

She raised her eyebrows at his tone. 'Inviting you?'

She was relieved to see the hint of a grin crease his mouth. 'Okay, manipulating me.'

She bit her lip, refusing to let her smile peek through. 'Manipulate is a strong word.'

His grey eyes locked on hers. 'Lucky I didn't use it then.'

She shook her head, unable to help the smile that broke out. 'Always so pedantic, aren't you?'

He moved closer. 'Well, were you manipulating me or not? 'Cause I seem to remember something like, Pleeeease Chase, it's a long way and I don't want to fall asleep driving and what if I need your help with Regal Zion? What if he goes wild and smashes his way out of the horse trailer? You don't want us both killed, do you? Imagine the world without us in it.'

He was exaggerating. His eyes held a playful challenge and she laughed but it stuck in her throat. It was then that it struck her. She loved him. Deeply. She wanted to be with him like this, always. The knowledge jarred her so greatly she couldn't think. She couldn't tear her gaze away. His grey eyes were holding hers, waiting for an answer. She faltered.

'Um, what was your question again?'

He chuckled low in his throat. 'Manipulation, remember? I'm trying to work out who is manipulating who right now.'

She hadn't meant to manipulate him, but she desperately wanted him with her on this trip. She swallowed hard. 'I do need company to keep me awake and help with Regal Zion on the journey. But I think it will be good for you to see where he's going; to see the reunion and say goodbye.'

'I don't like goodbyes. I never have.'

His tone was filled with meaning and Starre found a tight lump forming in her throat. What would happen once Regal Zion was returned to Prince? Would she ever see Chase again? She watched as he closed the back of the horse float and moved to the passenger side of the car. She checked Regal Zion one more time, then moved to the driver's seat.

Bruce waved them off and they were on their way. She glanced at Chase, stunned by the intensity of her feelings for him. She loved his good nature. She loved his warm heart. She loved everything about him. Even with his scars he was a good looking man. Prince had confided in her that he'd like Paul Seton to act as Chase in the re-enactment of their story for the documentary. She agreed Paul was a good match. His fair hair and tall, good looks were appropriate.

'I just wish he had grey eyes like you.'

She spoke the words before she'd thought properly. Chase's eyes flew to hers. 'Who? What?'

She laughed at herself. 'Sorry. Just thinking out loud. I know Paul is a good choice to act the part of you, but he doesn't have grey eyes.'

Chase smiled almost sadly. 'I hardly think the colour of my eyes is important.'

She disagreed but hesitated to voice her thoughts. Was it worth putting her heart on the line? Finally she gathered up her courage and said softly, 'But I love your grey eyes. It was the first thing I recognised when I saw you again after all these years.'

If he heard, he didn't respond. Had she made him uncomfortable? That was the last thing she wanted to do. She'd have to be more careful about expressing all that was going on in her heart.

Their first stop was two hours later. Chase had slept some of the time, but he now stretched and climbed out of the car before going to Regal Zion. He opened the back of the float and led the horse out. Starre put some water in a bucket and watched him drink. Chase stood slightly to the side, watching. After a short drink, Regal Zion moved between the two of them, throwing his head over Chase's shoulder and then Starre's.

Starre laughed as he nudged her toward Chase. 'Stop it.'

Chase grinned. 'He's got the right idea.' He threw his arm over her shoulder and drew her closer. Joy filled her as she looked up at him. He was back to his old, cheerful self. But just as quickly he pulled back.

She studied him. 'What's wrong?'

He put his hands in his pockets and looked down at his feet. 'Soon the whole country is going to see just how amazing you are, Starre. You were made to be admired. Your whole family always were. It was only a matter of time.'

He was concerned about losing her? That was certainly what it sounded like. Could he feel the same way as she did? She took a deep breath and spoke. 'I don't want greatness if I can't share it with you.' She didn't know what gave her the courage to speak the words. Maybe it was the fear of losing him again. Maybe it was the sadness in his eyes.

He shook his head. 'You always were too good for me. I mean, look at you. You were meant for greatness.'

She frowned. 'The only true greatness I should have attained I threw away. I never forgave. I never let God heal my hurts and I never sought the truth.' Her lower lip trembled as she reached a hand and touched the side of his face. 'You showed true greatness, Chase. You gave everything up for others. You stood up for what's right.'

He blinked hard, then reached his large hand to cover hers. She ran her thumb along the scars down his cheek but he moved her hand. 'Just look at me, Starre.'

She looked. Her heart welled with love and tenderness. 'All I see are marks of loyalty and sacrifice.'

He caught his breath, then reached out to hold either side of her face in his hands. His gaze was warm. 'You mean that, don't you?'

She nodded, overwhelmed by all she saw in his clear grey eyes. 'I love you. I never forgave you all those years ago because it would hurt too much if I did and found I still loved you. But I do. Even after all these years.'

He blinked hard, then licked his lips. She studied them, remembering how it had felt to be kissed by those lips as a teenager. It had taken her breath away. She'd thought there could be nothing like it in all the world. He'd been gentle and uncertain.

'Kiss me again?' she whispered.

His eyes questioned her before he came closer. Regal Zion shoved his head between them. With a chuckle, he gently pushed the horse away. He seemed to get the hint and stayed perfectly still.

Then Chase kissed her for the second time in fifteen years. Only this time it was clear he knew what he was doing. Warm and confident, his lips claimed hers in a way that left her wanting more.

'It's been way too long,' he murmured, his lips still against hers.

'It has.'

He moved back far enough to look into her eyes, then chuckled deep in his throat as she locked her arms around his neck and pulled him closer so that he would kiss her again.

'Pushy, aren't you?' His eyes twinkled before he titled his head and kissed her, this time with complete abandon. And she felt no fear, no hurt, no regrets about the past. She only felt blessed and overwhelmed with love for this man.

This is more than forgiveness. This is grace.

Regal Zion's nudge interrupted them and they stepped back from one another. Chase laughed as he rubbed the horse's nose. 'For the first time I don't have regrets about giving you back to Prince. But good luck to him if he tries to kiss his wife with you around!'

He led Regal Zion back to the float, sending a grin toward Starre. 'As much as I'd like to stay here and enjoy more of the same, we'd better get going, unless you want to be the one to explain to your family why we're late.'

Starre grinned too. The old Chase was back. Maybe God had already answered her prayer and granted his deepest desires.

***

Sky's phone beeped and she scooped it up from her bedside table. Jake. He'd finally got himself a phone and learned to text.

I can't wait to see you tomorrow, he texted. She'd have to teach him how to abbreviate. He always did everything so properly! With a grin, she texted back.

Who r u? Do I know u?

She began packing her bag and within moments her phone beeped again. She smiled as she read his text.

Not nearly well enough.

She pressed his number. She desperately wanted to hear his voice. It didn't take long for him to answer and she knew he had been holding his phone.

'Jake Timms here. Whom do I have the pleasure of speaking with?'

There was laughter in his voice and she chuckled. 'Jake. My name is Sky Clements. I don't know if you remember me, but I used to go to camps with you.'

There was a pause, then she heard him take in a breath, pretending to be in shock. 'Sky. Yes, now I remember. How are you?'

'Well. I think. Um, do you have a girlfriend?'

He laughed. 'Now that's a very personal question.'

'I know. It's just I think you should know that I admire you and your relationship with God and I'd like to develop a more serious type of relationship with you.'

She heard him take another breath, then he chuckled. 'Sounds good to me. But what would you do if I did happen to have a girlfriend already?'

Sky smiled at the way he went along with her. She'd once thought he lacked a sense of humour. How wrong she had been.

'Sky, you there?'

She came back to the present. 'Yeah, just thinking. Enjoying being with you.'

She could picture the laugh lines around his mouth and the sparkle in his eyes. 'I'm sure there's cheaper ways to be together. I hope you have a good mobile plan.'

Bonnie poked her head in the door and Sky shrugged a little guiltily before mouthing the name 'Jake' to explain. Bonnie raised her eyebrows and Sky laughed. 'Actually, I'd better go. Mum's giving me the look. See you tomorrow?'

'I'm counting on it. I love you. Bye.'

Sky couldn't quite get out the words 'I love you,' before he was gone. Bonnie was still in the doorway and Sky grinned at her. 'Sorry. Just had to talk to him.'

Bonnie rolled her eyes, then smiled. 'I know. I feel like that most of the day when Blaze is at work.'

'Mum, were you madly in love with Dad? When you first saw him did you know he was the one?'

Bonnie chuckled, lowering herself onto the bed. 'No. I was interested in him, just like I was any potential friend, but as for being swept away, it was nothing like that. Blaze's face was covered in teenage pimples and he seemed to get nervous every time I showed him any kind of affection. I guess I gradually grew to love him.'

Sky smiled. 'I guess I just gradually grew to love Jake, too. But I thought it had to be …'

'Dramatic?' Bonnie supplied.

Sky nodded.

'No. In fact, I've heard the best relationships develop as friendships first.'

Sky looked down, fingering the folds in the blanket on her bed. 'I thought I loved Paul Seton. I thought he was the one I'd spend my life with because whenever I saw him I'd get this excitement; a kind of emotional rush. But when it comes down to it, he doesn't even know or respect me.'

Bonnie came and sat beside her. 'He hurt you?'

She raised her eyes. 'He was awful, Mum. I've never been so hurt and humiliated in my life. Then he was sorry and I knew I should forgive him. I did, but then he wanted me to kiss him and … well, he hurt me again. He has no idea about me or who I really am.'

Bonnie took her face in her hands and her blue eyes connected with hers. 'Sky, you're only young. You can't know that anyone is the one for you. Not long term.'

Sky bit her lip. 'But I can at least begin developing relationships.'

'You can, but it doesn't have to be as serious as potential marriage.'

Sky nodded. 'I know.'

Bonnie smiled and gave her a hug. 'I'm not ready to give you up yet, my daughter. And the man who finally wins your heart had better be pretty special before I'm willing to let you go.'

'Like Jake? '

Bonnie smiled wider. 'I have to admit I like him. But let's just wait and see.'

Bonnie left and Sky continued packing. She chuckled as she packed the same clock she'd taken to camp last time. She remembered Jake's face when he'd realised his clocks had been changed. He was a good sport. He always had been, even back when he had been infatuated with her and become so nervous he couldn't have a normal conversation. She'd liked the idea that he was so taken with her, but never considered anything more. She'd been waiting for a dream like Paul Seton to come along.

'I was a fool.' She let out a sigh. 'How ironic that it took Paul to wake me up.'

Her dream of Paul had been nicer than the reality. But Jake was more special than any girlish dream she'd imagined.

***

It felt strange to arrive at Camp Oaken to a mostly empty car park. Sky was used to it being busy and noisy as campers arrived or departed from another camp. It was also hard to come to terms with the fact that her biological father and his family now lived and worked there. Charles and Marion had been talking about getting horses for a long time and Sky had been excited by the idea. She'd never imagined her own father would be the one to work with them.

The family had taken up the old caretaker's residence. The previous caretaker had five children and had used his spare time to renovate and extend the home. It was now more than large enough to hold Prince and his family.

Paul was the first person to greet them as they came to the front door. Sky felt humiliation burn her cheeks.

'Hey, Uncle Blaze, Aunt Bonnie,' he welcomed them. Then his serious brown eyes met Sky's. 'Sky, I need to talk to you if you have a minute.'

She flinched, but he held her gaze unwaveringly. 'Please?'

Everything inside screamed to run from him but she managed a nod.

Bonnie's eyes met hers, searching for an excuse to stay by her side. But Sky knew she needed to sort things out with Paul. Alone. Seeming satisfied, Bonnie gave her shoulder a comforting squeeze. 'We'll head inside to see Prince and Rachel. See you both shortly.'

Sky was left looking at Paul. He now looked as uncomfortable as she felt. He moved his hand toward an outdoor table setting. 'Can we sit?'

She did, but chose a chair quite a distance from the one he sat in.

She watched the way he twisted his hands together in an agitated way. He swallowed a few times before looking directly at her. 'Sky, I know I've said sorry, but sorry isn't enough.'

Her eyes widened in surprise. That hadn't really been what she was expecting.

'I've spent some time with Kathina this week. Her family helped us with packing and moving. I've also talked quite a bit with Charles and Marion, people who know you way better than I do. I was totally wrong about you.'

It was there that Sky cut him off. 'Not totally wrong. You

saw my pride and resentment for what it was even before I did. God used you to show me a lot of things about myself.'

Paul winced. 'I don't think it was God who used me.'

'It think it was. If you hadn't humiliated me like that I might still be the same. I might never have seen myself for what I really am. I might never have forgiven my father.'

'But Sky, I didn't need to hurt you like that.' He groaned. 'I was so harsh. And you're not really the girl I thought you were.'

Sky studied him. It was true he hadn't been loving or gentle toward her. His motives hadn't been good, but God had used it for good anyway. She met his eyes. 'You're forgiven. And I'm glad you changed your mind about me, but you were right in some ways.'

Paul looked pained. 'So can things ever be different between us? I mean, can you ever see me as a friend?'

Sky picked up a twig sitting on the table and began to snap it into pieces. 'I'm hoping so. Or my brother, anyway.'

'Brother?'

She nodded. 'I'll find that easier until I get to see the nicer side of you. I mean, I heard all these wonderful things about you. Kathina told me what you're really like. I know everyone loves and admires you, but all I've seen is the …'

'The awful side.' He gave a resigned sigh. 'I guess I'll just have to prove to you that I have another side.'

Sky shrugged. 'Even if you don't, you're forgiven and I choose to love you as my brother.'

Paul steadily gazed at her until she dropped her eyes. She wondered if he could read what she was thinking; that it was safer to see him as a brother. Then he would never dare try kissing her or gaining her affections again. She was glad for Kathina because she had such deep, romantic feelings for him. But Sky never could. Loving him romantically had been merely a fanstasy for her. Loving him as a brother could be a reality.

'Kathina is coming down for Joanna's court case,' he said.

'She is? What for?'

'Support.'

'I thought we weren't allowed to be part of it. The police just took our statements and that was enough.'

He smiled sheepishly. 'She's coming as support for me.'

'You're struggling?'

He looked down and picked up another twig, snapping it apart just as she had. 'Yes. I can't get Joanna off my mind. Dad said you'll probably have to do a victim impact statement to be read out at her hearing.' He leaned forward. 'Sky, I want you to understand that Joanna's crime was a reaction to the pain she's been through. It's so easy for someone to be tipped over the edge. What Joanna did to you wasn't personal. She's probably going to have to go into a juvenile detention centre. She will have counselling and a psychiatrist will work with her. But what you say could have a big effect. We don't know what will happen to her once she turns eighteen.'

He was speaking so fast that she had to hold out a hand to stop him.

'Paul, it's okay. I've forgiven her. She shouldn't have done it, but I'm okay. God used it for good in so many ways.'

His eyes searched hers. 'You mean that?'

She smiled. 'Yes. Thanks to you I understand a whole lot more about true forgiveness.'

He shook his head. 'No, thanks to God. Don't thank me for anything. Forgiveness is all I ask.'

It took everything she had, but she forced herself to stand and move toward him. 'Can I hug you? As a sister?'

His mouth curved up into a smile as he came and drew her into a quick, brotherly hug. 'Thank you,' he said, his voice husky.

She stepped back and grinned. 'I hope you realise being my brother means I can pick on you the way Seton and Blythe pick on each other.'

He quirked an eyebrow. 'I can take it. Bring it on.'

She chuckled, giving him a playful slap on the arm. 'You'll be sorry.'

'I doubt it.'

Laughing, she headed inside, her heart free. She wanted to dance and sing. If she did have to write a victim impact statement as Paul had said, she would have to state that she wasn't in fact a victim. True she was still working through it; she still had flashbacks of Joanna's attack, but the main impact had been to bring her closer to God and family and all those she loved.

Chapter Twenty-Seven

As soon as she entered the house, Sky's attention was drawn to where Jake stood in the corner of the room, watching the door. He came to her and drew her into his arms.

'Everything okay?' he asked down into her hair. She heard the beating of his heart and knew it was going as fast as hers. He smelled good. She didn't know what kind of deodorant he wore, but it was a familiar scent. Maybe he'd always worn it but she hadn't really noticed it until now. Funny how everything about him now seemed more distinct.

'It is now.'

'Good. I've missed you.' She loved the sound of his deep voice as she leaned her ear against his chest, his strong arms around her, the expressiveness of his eyes as she looked up to smile at him.

'I love you, Jake.' she said, unable to help herself.

He drew in a deep breath then grinned. 'I love you too.'

He pushed her toward the lounge room. 'You've got some family to meet. But then I want to show you something.'

She raised her brows, but he gave her a gentle shove. 'Meet your family. I'll see you later.'

She watched as he walked out the door, looking back one last time before he left. Then she turned to meet her family.

Starre watched as Chase led Regal Zion into the paddock at the back of the camp. He had a good, long drink before stretching his legs and galloped away, up the hill. Cameras were trained on him and Starre knew she would have to get used to it. Part of her wanted to keep these precious moments to herself and not share them with the world, but she knew it was worth the loss of privacy to be able to promote animal rescue and share the amazing things God had done in her family at the same time.

The producer nodded in satisfaction. 'Beautiful animal. Are we ready to bring Prince out yet?'

Chase nodded. 'I'll get him.'

Starre watched Regal Zion as they waited. To her annoyance, she was told to stand a certain way so the wind could catch her hair and the cameras could capture her watching Regal Zion. His proud stance and amazing colouring had her captivated as it always did. But there something special about him today. Almost as if he knew he was being watched and was performing.

Starre watched Prince approach. The cameras followed him and she knew the producer was impressed. Prince was made to be admired, with his dark good looks, his smooth flowing walk, his expressive face and dazzling smile.

He reached Starre and gave her a quick hug before giving a lopsided smile. 'I'm so nervous.'

'About the cameras?'

He shook his head. 'No. Regal Zion. What if he doesn't recognise me?'

'He recognised me.'

Prince's shoulders relaxed. 'He did, didn't he?' A new hope filled his eyes and she prayed that this reunion would be all they'd hoped it would be.

Make-up artists fussed over Prince but he seemed to take it

in his stride. She could see his eyes were straining up the hill to where Regal Zion was grazing, far in the distance.

'We're ready,' the producer called and Prince moved to the fence. Then he raised his fingers to his lips and blew out in a musical whistle. The moment he did, the horse's head jerked in their direction. Then it hurtled toward them at such speed that everyone gasped.

'No, Regal, slow down. You'll hurt yourself,' Prince called. He scrambled over the fence and raced to meet the horse. They met part way, and Prince threw his arms around his neck while the horse gave excited whinnies, throwing his head over one of Prince's shoulders and then the other.

Starre smiled at Regal Zion's familiar show of affection and joy. It was as though he couldn't get close enough. Then he gave a delighted snort and blew at Prince's dark hair. Watching from the fence, she wondered at how the two related as though they had never been apart.

'Well,' she said, a lump coming to her throat. 'What do you reckon? Did Regal Zion remember him?'

Someone laughed at her question. There was no need to answer it. Prince had tears pouring down his face as he led the horse over to the fence to meet them.

Starre moved to the paddock beside Regal Zion's and her eyes widened. There stood her sister Misty's horse, Victorian Dream. And beside her was Storm's horse, Dusty Lane. A moment of sadness overcame her as she thought of Steadfast Ever. She would have loved to have him here. Misty's husband Roy had provided her with a beautiful creature named Constant Shadow to play the part of Steadfast Ever, but she knew no horse could ever really take the place of her childhood friend.

'Feeling sad?'

She glanced up at Chase who had come and placed his arms around her from behind.

'A bit,' she admitted. 'But I'm so blessed too.'

***

The camp centre was full that night with members of the Clements family. The dining hall was the perfect place for them to have a meal together. The television crew sat around, interviewing different family members, consulting with Prince and working out how best to put the story together.

There were six family members to represent. Blaze, then the triplets, Starre, Prince and Misty, followed by the twins, Beauty and Storm. An actor had been brought in to play Blaze, but it was decided Sky would play a younger Starre. Seton would play Prince and Blythe would play Misty. Phillipa would be Beauty and Misty's son Benjamin would play Storm.

'You'll have to wear a long, messy black wig,' Storm told the boy with a grin. 'I was a grot, you know.'

Misty grinned at Storm. 'He won't need to practice the grot bit.'

Benjamin wrinkled his nose. 'Mum, that's not nice.'

Misty's husband Roy laughed. 'Or fair. I remember someone who was not quite so neat a few years back.' He gave Misty a meaningful look, then patted his son's shoulder. 'You'll do great, Ben.'

He put on a confident air. 'Of course I will. I'm a Clements.'

Sky laughed as she listened to the banter. Then she heard a car crunch the gravel outside the window. She didn't recognise the vehicle. It had P plates on the front. Could it be …?

She smiled as Jake got out. So this was what he had to show her. Escaping the noise of the room, she came out the door. She pointed to the car. 'You've got your licence. And a car?'

He nodded, pride in his eyes. 'I have. I've been saving for a while. I could have gone for my Ps way back but kept putting it off. I didn't really have anywhere to go. Until now.' He grinned at her. 'It will be great for coming to see you.'

He took her hand and led her to the car. 'It's pretty old and basic, but as long as it gets me to you, I don't care.'

He began showing it to her, describing each part as he did so, but all Sky was aware of was her hand in his. He had strong, manly hands. She felt secure and loved with him.

'So are you going to take me for a drive?' she asked, managing to focus on what he was telling her about how many kilometres the vehicle had travelled.

He smiled sheepishly. 'Hmm, that's not a good idea.'

Her eyebrows raised in question and he shrugged.

'Well, I've only just got my P plates and I find you quite distracting. Apart from that it's going to be hard to honour your wishes about not being kissed until you're sixteen if I have you alone in my car.'

A slight blush had coloured his cheeks and Sky grinned at him. Fair enough. She could accept his reasoning. She wouldn't tell him she would be sixteen next week.

'How about a walk, then?'

He nodded as he kept a hold on her hand and fumbled for the car keys in his pocket. He locked the car, then waved over toward the dining room. Sky followed his gaze and grinned when she saw Blaze looking out the window. She waved too, and Blaze nodded at them before looking down again.

'Do you think he trusts me?' Jake asked her with an amused lift of his brow.

Sky nodded. 'How could he not?'

They walked hand in hand until they reached the tree he so often sat under to read his Bible.

'Shall we sit?'

She grinned. 'Do you have a towel to sit on?'

'Nah. It's not early morning. There's no dew.'

They sat side by side and Jake gazed at her as though committing everything about her to memory. Then he leaned back against the tree and closed his eyes. Sky watched him, wishing she were game to reach up and touch his face. God had given her something special in this young man. To think she might have missed it because she was so focussed on being 'in love at first sight'.

He opened his eyes to find her gazing at him, her lips parted in a smile.

'What's that look for?'

She smiled wider. 'I'm just thinking there's a lot to be said for love at second sight.'

He nodded and leaned toward her, his eyes twinkling. 'And third and fourth and fifth … and millionth too, I hope.'

'You'll be doing a lot of driving, then.'

He came closer and rubbed his nose against hers in an affectionate way. 'No, I'm thinking I might have to kiss you soon so you have to marry me. That will save a lot of travelling time!'

His eyes were laughing as she moved back away from him. 'That's not quite how it works, Jake.'

He pretended to look disappointed, but drew her back to his side where he sat with his arm around her and his eyes closed again.

'Some moments should last forever,' he said lazily. 'I think this is a bit of a taste of heaven.'

Sky agreed with him. Even the grass seemed greener as she sat there with Jake beneath the large old tree. She would be happy to sit there with him forever.

They sat that way for several minutes before Jake's deep voice interrupted her thoughts. 'So when's the official adoption going through?'

'Blaze got the paperwork. I think he got Prince to sign it last night. I just have to sign it now.'

'What are you waiting for?'

Sky bit her lip. 'I don't know. It just scares me. What if I disappoint them? What if I let them down?'

'Everyone lets someone down at some time in their lives. True love goes deeper than that.'

She sighed. 'I know. But I have this fear I can't seem to get rid of. Sometimes I find it hard to believe that God even loves me, now that I've realised just how selfish and human I really am.'

Jake's eyes turned intense as they bored into hers. 'So when that happens, do you tell Satan to get lost?'

'Um, no.'

He took her hand. 'Better still, remember Jesus. Don't even give the devil the satisfaction of a thought. Jesus died for you. He must hate it when we doubt his love and don't accept his forgiveness. All he ever wanted was for us to be part of his family; his beloved children.'

That was all Blaze and Bonnie wanted from her too. She stood and reached a hand to help Jake up. 'Come on, I have to go sign those papers.'

The laugh lines around Jake's eyes deepened. 'Just like that.'

'Just like that.'

Prince sat on one side of Sky as she studied the adoption papers, Blaze and Bonnie on the other. Jake sat across; her silent support. She turned troubled eyes to Prince. 'You really don't mind?'

He smiled his dazzling smile. 'You'll always be my daughter and I'll always love you, but Blaze and Bonnie have been your real parents since you were tiny. I don't mind.'

Jake grinned across at her. 'So there you go. Do it! Do the official part.'

She stared down at the papers, then with a glance into Blaze and Bonnie's shining eyes, gripped the pen in her shaking fingers. Once the pen touched the paper, all hesitation left. With a laugh of triumph, she finished her signature and threw down the pen before jumping up into Blaze and Bonnie's waiting arms.

Prince then held her tight for several moments before looking down at her, obvious love in his eyes. 'Thank you for letting me be part of something so special.'

'Yeah,' came Jakes voice from beside her. 'I can tell people I witnessed Sky Clements become Sky Clements.'

His eyes were twinkling, and Sky playfully hit his arm. Then she turned to Blaze and Bonnie. 'I love you so much. Thanks for being my parents.'

Jake looked to Blaze. 'So she'll have to call you dad, now.'

Sky chuckled at him. 'You're always so practical, aren't you? I've been calling him dad since camp.'

Jake's eyes widened. 'Ever since you met your real dad?'

She nodded. 'I know. Ironic, isn't it?'

He shook his head. 'No, special. More evidence of the way God miraculously works in people.' Then he looked directly at Blaze. 'I'm hoping to be there the next time she changes her name too. In fact, I'm hoping to be the cause of it.'

Blaze merely smiled at Jake. 'I'm expecting it to happen, Jake, but maybe you should wait until she's at least eighteen.'

He screwed up his face. 'That's a long time to wait. Do we have to wait until we're eighteen to become engaged?'

Blaze laughed at Jake's eagerness. 'Please at least let her be my daughter for a while first. You can have her later.'

Sky smiled at their conversation and came to put her arms around Blaze. 'I'll always be your daughter, Dad. Even when I'm married. Besides, you've always been my dad, really. I always knew you loved me. Even when I was fostered out, whenever you looked at me I knew you loved me.'

Tears were sparkling in Blaze's eyes as he held her tightly. She looked to Bonnie. Nothing could hide the joy in her bright blue eyes. Sky felt as though she truly had just come home. Now she belonged.

CHAPTER TWENTY-EIGHT

Sky sat between Blaze and Jake, gazing up at the large television screen in the camp hall. The documentary was finished and ready for approval from the family before it went to air. Even the crew had been amazed at how well it all came together and the powerful story it told. Old footage of the six Clements children performing in the ring was found in Marcos' circus archives. Sky had heard the stories many times, but she was blown away by the appearance of the majestic horses and their skilful riders.

'You really were amazing, Dad,' she said in Blaze's ear as the footage was played. She watched as he stood on the back of his moving horse wearing his captain's costume and leading the way. Behind him were Starre and Misty dressed as princesses. Then came the regal Prince dressed as a prince, Beauty dressed as a fairy, and Storm as Peter Pan.

They rode around the big top, impressing people with their appearance alone, before awing them with their spectacular performance on the magnificent horses. She could almost feel the adrenaline and the applause was so loud Sky was amazed the horses didn't start. Yet it was clear they were born performers. Their poise and grace were breathtaking.

The Clements family sat, their eyes glued to the television screen as the story played out.

'And you gave all this up for God?' the presenter was now

asking Blaze.

Blaze nodded. 'Yes. The world saw us as amazing performers, but God saw us as his children. He chased us down until each of us surrendered our lives to him.'

'Chased you down?' the presenter asked. 'What do you mean by that?'

Blaze told them about Bonnie and the fire that almost took her life. A re-enactment was shown, then Blaze was speaking again. 'It taught us the value of human life above that of our horses.'

Bonnie then stood beside him and willingly showed the cameras the remains of her scars from that terrible day.

'But God used it,' she told the presenter, joy and peace radiating from her bright blue eyes. 'If I hadn't been burned I would never have recognised my mortality and searched for answers.'

'And Blaze, you almost died too,' the presenter said, turning back to him. 'You lost your horse to tetanus and it almost took your life as well?'

Blaze nodded, and then Misty appeared with Victorian Dream by her side as she told the story of how he almost died and how that had caused her to search for God in the bid to know about life after death.

'And you, Beauty, lost your horse in a horrific accident that also stole the life of a child,' the presenter said, turning to her. She nodded, and tears filled her eyes as she spoke of the guilt she had felt over the accident and over her own mother's death. She told how God had shown her his forgiveness and she had been set free from the guilt.

Then finally, the miracle of Prince and Regal Zion being reunited was shown. The scene was re-enacted, with Prince whistling to the horse high up on the hill. This time Regal Zion, his coat glossy and healthy, galloped down the hill at break-neck speed and into Prince's arms.

As it finished, a song was played; a song Prince's wife Rachel had written and which Paul sang with her. The soulful sound of their voices filled the room and no one spoke.

You are so, so loved, why can't you see it?
You perform so well, yes you hide your heart,
As you strive for hope in a broken world,
That has told you lies from the very start.

So here I stand, reaching out my hands,
Can't you see the scars, can't you understand
That I died for you just the way you are,
Longing for your love, for your life, your heart?

You are so, so loved, why can't you see it?
You expect much more than I've asked of you,
Won't you let it go and look in my eyes,
All my love is there, it will see you through.

So here you are, in my arms secure,
And the whole lost world watches on in awe,
For you are my child, dearly loved always
Living in my hope, learning all my ways.

The song ended and credits rolled. All sat staring at the screen. Sky knew that God had truly brought about miracles in their lives.

She looked at Starre. What had begun as a way to bring publicity to an animal rescue centre God had changed to share the great story of how he'd stepped in and showed a lost circus family his forgiveness and love.

Chapter Twenty-Nine

Starre stood watching Chase with Regal Zion. He seemed back to his normal self, but he still didn't know what he was going to do when he returned home.

A figure was heading across the paddock toward them, and Starre smiled. Alexa had taken a real liking to him. He had a way with troubled teens.

'She wants to know more about the possible outcomes of Joanna's court case,' Chase had told Starre the night before. 'I was able to explain it all to her. I think it helped.'

Alexa was now in earnest conversation with him again and she knew the girl just needed to talk. The court case was taking place that day and Prince and Rachel had gone to support Joanna.

Alexa's laugh floated across the breeze and Starre felt warmth fill her heart. Even if he couldn't chase criminals and fight gunmen, Chase still had a purpose in this world.

Show him what you have for him, Lord.

Even as she prayed it struck her. Chase would be perfect in a camp centre like this one. He loved young people and he loved horses. He had an air of authority about him that even troubled teenagers responded to. And Regal Zion was here.

But the camp centre couldn't afford him. They were struggling as it was and they might even have to close down.

God, is there a way?

'They're back. It's all over.'

Sky looked up at Jake from where she had been sitting beneath the old elm tree, praying. 'How did it go?'

He reached a hand to help her up. 'I'm not sure. Prince and Rachel want us all to meet in the hall and they'll let us know.'

She walked by his side. 'Oh Jake, I'm scared.'

His eyes shot to hers. 'Why? She'll be locked up. She'll never hurt you again.'

Sky gave a half laugh. 'I'm not scared *of* her. I'm scared *for* her. I don't want her locked up.'

'What? She was going to kill you!'

Jake sounded incredulous. She could tell he was working at calming himself. She waited and finally he let out a deep sigh. 'Sorry. I just … I can't bear to think of what she did to you, and here you are not just forgiving her, but worrying about her. Now that's grace!'

'Maybe. But I do know there are reasons for the way she is. All of us have reasons for the way we are. We all have a sinful human nature. Some of us are pushed to the edge while others don't go through enough trauma to draw it out.'

Jake seemed to be considering what she was saying. Then she heard the smile in his voice. 'Okay then, you've convinced me. I'll try to forgive her too. But if she comes near you, I'll be keeping a very close eye on her.'

Sky laughed. 'You don't have to be my hero.'

He put on a gruff voice. 'Yes, I do. I intend to always stick by your side. Then if someone tries to kill you again I can be the hero like I should have been last time.'

'Oh, Jake,' She let out a giggle. 'You're always a hero to me.'

'Yeah, that's right,' he agreed. 'I remember saving you from getting wet once. I think you were going to sit on the wet ground or something. Hmm, maybe I should bring a towel wherever I go.'

'And wear it like a cape around your shoulders.'

He let out a laugh. 'Now that, my Sky, would be going too far!'

She drank in the sound of his laugh. She would never tire of hearing it.

They made their way into the meeting room where Prince and Rachel stood before the group. Chairs scraped as everyone found a seat.

Prince cleared his throat. 'It's been a difficult day. Joanna didn't express any remorse. She will be sentenced next month, but it's almost certain she'll be spending the rest of her teen years in juvenile detention.'

Sky pictured the petite, subdued Joanna and a lump came to her throat. It was hard to believe she was a murderer.

'The defence argued that she was a girl driven by desperation; trapped in a situation with no way out. When no one believed what she suffered at the hands of her mother's de-facto, she did the only thing she could think of doing. It was self-preservation.'

Rachel spoke, then. 'But the judge found there was no excuse for the way she attacked Alexa and Sky.'

Alexa jumped up and she looked near to tears. 'I thought I drove her to it. I thought the way I kept pretending I was going to commit suicide made her do it.'

Then Chase was there. 'No, Alexa, it wasn't your fault. Justice is being served.'

Alexa's eyes did fill with tears, then. 'I think it was easier to blame myself than it will be to forgive her.'

Understanding filled Sky and Chase obviously understood, too. He drew Alexa aside and his words were gentle and reassuring. 'Forgiveness is a continual choice. God will help you. Every time you feel angry, hand it back to God.'

Alexa nodded, appearing calmer despite her tears. 'Because Jesus forgave me.'

Sky felt tears come to her own eyes. Alexa truly was a

Clements now. Joanna could have been too, if she hadn't chosen to react the wrong way to her pain. If only she'd turned to God and accepted him as her Heavenly Father. And if only she'd allowed Prince and Rachel to adopt her. Instead, she'd be facing years alone in a detention centre, belonging to nobody.

Everyone stood, and Sky gazed out the window. She didn't know what to think or feel. Then she noticed Kathina was at the back of the room. Paul was beside her. She smiled. Kathina would always be there if someone needed support. It seemed clear she'd forgiven Paul and that their friendship was restored.

'Thanks, God,' she found herself praying. 'Please work it all out for them.'

Then her mouth fell open, for Paul reach for Kathina and drew her into a hug. Then his mouth lowered as he gave her a slow, gentle kiss. It was nothing like the quick peck he'd placed on her own lips a few weeks back.

'What's up?' Jake asked, following her gaze to the back of the room. His eyes widened too, as he caught the last of the kiss. He let out a chuckle as he reached a hand to turn her head away. 'Don't stare. They might think we saw that.'

Sky couldn't help laughing with him. 'Saw what? A miracle?'

He smiled down at her. 'A miracle? Now this is a miracle having you here with me, holding my hand and looking at me like you love me.'

Sky pretended to look shocked. 'Did I look at you like I loved you? I'll have to be more careful.'

He screwed up his face at her and she chuckled as she put her arms around him. 'You really are astute, though. It's true. I love you.'

Kathina was waiting outside to catch up with Sky. She came to her with a cry of delight and they hugged. She drew her to the side while the others talked.

'Sky, I've got something to tell you,' she said, and her whole face glowed with happiness.

She grinned. 'Is it anything to do with what I saw going on inside a few minutes ago?'

Kathina blushed a deep scarlet and Sky let out a laugh. 'Must be.'

She nodded, looking uncomfortable. 'I'm sorry you saw that. I hope I haven't disappointed you.'

Now Sky was confused. 'Kathina, I don't have feelings for Paul.'

'No, not that. I know the standards you have about kissing. I've always admired you for refusing to kiss a guy until you knew you were going to marry him. But it's not like I have lots of boyfriends like you. In fact, I've never had one before now and I don't plan to have another one.'

Sky laughed. 'You don't owe me an explanation. I never meant to enforce my standards on other people. I just told you about mine so you could help keep me accountable.'

She looked surprised, then giggled. 'Oh. Okay, I take all that back.'

Sky giggled too, her eyes bright. 'So tell me, what happened between you two?'

Kathina cast a shy glance in Paul's direction. 'I forgave him like you said I should. And he realised that he ...' she blushed deeper, 'that he's attracted to me. He's always been the type to look deeper than the skin. But he says he likes the way I look anyway.'

Sky grinned. 'Of course he does. You've gone the most gentle, friendly, smiling face I've ever seen. You're the sweetest, most Christlike friend I've ever had.'

Tears filled the girl's eyes, but they sparkled with joy. 'Thank you, Sky,' she whispered. 'I think the same about you.'

The two hugged again and Sky knew so much joy she thought she would burst. God had worked things out perfectly for all of them. He was continually teaching them, maturing them, guiding them. He would never leave her or forsake her. He was always there.

CHAPTER THIRTY

Jake sat with his head in his hands beneath the large old elm tree. Sky lowered herself beside him. 'What's up?'

He shook his head. 'Just praying for this place; for its future.'

'Things still aren't good?'

He sighed. 'I don't know. Having Prince here with the horses should make a difference, but Mum and Dad have never been good at finances. They're great with cooking and camp leading, but … I don't want to leave any of this. It would break my heart to see the camp centre fold. But we don't have the workers or the money to keep it going.'

Sky looked around. She knew what he meant. She loved it too. God had used this place in her life. No, not the place; the people. Despite the fact that she shared Jake's sadness over it, she looked around and her heart fell full. Her family were all there. The earthly family who loved her, whom God had given her.

Down by the horse yards, Chase was talking to Alexa. He had so much experience with children from troubled backgrounds and understood the law and justice system. Alexa looked relaxed and happy as he spoke to her.

She looked to where Blaze sat at the picnic tables with his Bible open, his face animated as he pointed out a verse to Charles and Marion. They were nodding, their expressions earnest. Blaze worked as a youth pastor, encouraging young people to walk with

God. Bonnie supported him in that role, God's love shining through her brilliant blue eyes. She was also a nurse, up to date in first aid.

Sky then looked to Rachel, who sat beside Paul. He was strumming along on his guitar. Rachel was a psychologist and musician. Paul, also a gifted musician, was experienced with teaching children to ride horses and reaching out to people with troubled pasts.

A child's laughter floated across the room and her attention was drawn to Misty. Misty sat with a puppet on her hand, entertaining the children. Roy was laughing too, as he spoke with the puppet.

A shout from the horse yard caught her attention. She looked over. The horses Roy and Misty had bred were being led around the yard by Seton. But on the back of one of them stood Prince. Storm was encouraging him, reminding him how to do a backflip. He then jumped up onto the horse and demonstrated. Tori was looking up at him and Sky remembered that Tori was an accountant who had managed the finances of a whole circus. Tori had also been abused as a child but had overcome the hurt and grown to understand the love of God.

Starre was studying Regal Zion's leg, checking it was completely healed. Her vet nurse and animal rescue skills were invaluable in a place like this.

Sky looked around. Where were Beauty and Chappy? She should have known. Chappy was studying a dying elm tree by the side of the building, his brow furrowed. Beauty was by his side, pointing to one of the dead branches. Landscape gardeners.

It was then it struck her. Here were the exact people this camp needed. Their life experiences, their training, their gifts … it was as though God had set up them up for such a time as this.

She could see it. Their whole family working together, the camp centre full. Foster children coming to find hope, healing and love. School groups coming in for recreational camps but hearing about God at the same time. Adults coming to learn and grow in their love and knowledge of God. Tired missionaries and their families coming for a break from their overseas or full time ministry work.

And the Clements family ministering to them, teaching them to ride horses, teaching them to swim and dive, providing a place of hope and joy.

What was the name of Regal Zion's mother? Hope of Zion.

Suddenly Prince was at her side. He was breathing hard, his face flushed. 'Sky, look at us.' He waved his hand around at the scene before him.

She nodded. 'Hope of Zion. That's what this place needs to be called. God's place where all his people learn to live in peace, in his love. Hope of heaven.'

Prince's dark eyes widened and connected with hers before his mouth stretched into a smile. 'I had a vision while I was standing there on the back of that horse, trying to recapture my past. A vision of the future and how the past fits into it.'

Sky grinned. 'I know. I saw it too.'

Jake waved his arms in front of their faces, his brow furrowed. 'Hey, wait a minute. You're both obviously on the same page, but you've lost me. Fill me in.'

She couldn't. Her heart was beating hard, excitement and joy overwhelming her. Prince's eyes shone and she knew he felt the same.

He glanced around. 'I think we need to call a family meeting. We'll explain it then.'

Sky grinned at Jake's perplexed expression. She had just connected with her biological father in a way she never would have imagined she could. God had given them both the same vision, the same hope, the same gift. She gave him a spontaneous hug. 'Let's do it.'

***

Starre listened as Sky and Prince shared their vision with them all.

202

She sensed the excitement around her and felt it too. It couldn't be chance, could it, that they were all gifted and experienced for such a place as this?

She hated to put a dampener on it all, but there was one thing they weren't thinking about. 'Where would we all live?'

Prince shrugged. 'I haven't thought that far. In town, maybe? We could find rental properties to begin with until the camp centre builds up enough money to house us all.'

Starre frowned. 'That could be years.'

'Or never.' Marion's subdued voice added.

But Charles let out a laugh and stood. 'Come on, people. Who can provide us all we need? Who owns the horses on a thousand hills?'

'Cattle, Dad. It's cattle.'

He grinned at Jake. 'I know son, just being relevant.' He looked out at everybody. 'Are you all willing? Do you all have a feeling in your hearts that this would work?'

Everyone nodded.

'So let's pray about it. Let's trust God to provide.'

Starre glanced to her side, sensing that Chase was watching her. When she met his eyes, he leaned close. 'If this goes ahead and we all live here, I'm going to marry you. You know that, don't you?'

She did. She could see it in his eyes. The way he looked at her with such love left her overwhelmed.

Please God, provide a way for us all to live and work here. Her silent prayer was more heartfelt than anyone else's.

CHAPTER THIRTY-ONE

The day came for the story to be aired on national television. Sky wasn't sure if she liked all the media attention and the busyness it brought to their lives, but she could see the joy it brought to the six Clements siblings.

They saw it not only as an opportunity to relive their past and reunite with each other and the horses still alive, but to tell the story of the difference God had made in all their lives.

The presenters were talking with Prince about making a movie about the whole story.

'It's a bit scary to think you might become famous,' Jake told her as they sat around the lunch table.

'Why?' Sky asked with a teasing smile. 'Scared I'll become rich and famous and forget you? Or people will be so captivated by my beauty that I'll be stalked by every guy in the country?'

'Yeah, that must be it.' He poked her in the ribs and she giggled.

Blaze and Bonnie smiled at their playfulness. Then a thoughtful look came to Bonnie's eyes. 'You know, Jake, I have an idea.' She glanced sideways at Blaze before continuing. 'I remember a handsome teenager once worrying about his looks. I fixed it with a good dose of manure.'

'Hey!' Blaze cut in. 'I stopped you, remember? You tried, but I was too strong for you.'

Bonnie shrugged and grinned impishly. 'Maybe. I don't

remember the details. But my point is, if you're worried about the world being taken with Sky's beauty, there's a sure way to fix it.'

Sky's mouth rounded as she stared in disbelief at Bonnie. 'Mum! How could you even suggest that to him?'

Jake was already standing, looking out the window toward the horse paddock. 'There must be plenty of manure out there with all those horses.'

Sky stood, too. 'No, Jake! Seriously, it's not funny. All my relatives are about to arrive to watch the documentary on live television. It's going to be a special moment.'

'Exactly.'

His eyes sparkled dangerously and she backed away. 'You wouldn't dare!'

'Dare?' Jake asked, quirking an eyebrow. 'You had my sympathy until you used that word. It's now a challenge. Sorry, Sky, I have no choice.'

'You do,' she began, but she saw his look and ran. She heard Blaze and Bonnie's laughter behind her, but more concerning was the sound of Jake's feet pounding close at her heels.

She ran for a while, but she knew he hadn't had time to collect any manure, so she slowed. Within seconds he'd caught her and pinned her tightly against his chest. She struggled against him and turned so that she was facing him and smiled up into his eyes. She didn't really believe he would carry out his threat, especially when he was looking at her the way he was. He drew in a deep breath and his expression was tender. It was as though he couldn't draw his gaze away.

'What? She felt the colour rising in her cheeks.

'Sometimes it's hard to honour your wishes,' he admitted, 'because right now I want to kiss you so badly it hurts.'

Sky let out a giggle. 'It hurts that you want to kiss me or hurts that I'm too fast for you?'

'Too fast?' He laughed. 'If you're so fast, what are you doing here in my arms?'

She grinned up at him. 'Have you ever thought that this might be exactly where I want to be?'

He looked upward for a moment, pretending to consider what she had said. She remembered back to when she had thought he was too serious. How wrong she'd been.

When he looked back down at her, he was no longer laughing. His eyes were filled with longing and she knew he was struggling.

'Jake,' she warned breathlessly as his head lowered toward hers, 'you do that and you have to marry me.'

He smiled softly as he moved even closer. 'That's the best incentive I've had to kiss you yet.'

She didn't want to resist him, but she wasn't sure what to do. His warm breath blew against her skin. Before she could decide, his lips had met hers. He was gentle, but she sensed his passion and desire. She felt it too.

His hand came to the back of her neck and he moved to explore further.

'Wait,' Sky pleaded half-heartedly, pushing him back, both hands against his chest.

He drew in a deep breath, then let out a low moan. 'You were so wise, Sky. You knew didn't you, that one kiss would never be enough?'

She nodded. 'Not when it's the right one.'

Jake reached his hand and ran his knuckles down her face. Then he stepped back. He was studying her and she knew he was deep in thought. She waited to see if he would share what was making him look so serious.

'I always wondered about Paul,' he confessed. 'Was it like ours, the kiss?'

Sky almost laughed. 'No. Nothing like it. It was a quick peck that felt like … well, nothing.'

He quirked an eyebrow. 'Seriously?'

'Seriously. He looked so shocked when I said I'd never kissed anyone before that he just froze.'

Jake grinned. 'So, him having the wrong idea about you actually saved you for me?'

Sky nodded thoughtfully. 'I guess you're right. Hmm, it was worth all that pain.'

Jake didn't say anything more. He took her hand and led her back to the horse yards. Sky knew he was removing himself from temptation and she respected him for it.

As they approached the yard, Jake stopped. He turned to face her again. 'I'm for real. Do you understand that?'

She nodded, seeing the sincerity in his eyes. The thing about Jake was that he was always for real.

'I mean, I want to marry you. I want to buy a ring, ask your dad … all the right things.'

She threw her arms around him, squeezing him tightly. 'Yes, Jake. When I'm old enough I'll marry you.'

His perplexed expression disappeared and a grin lit up his face. 'You will?'

'Do you think I would have let you kiss me if I wasn't planning to marry you?'

'Good point.'

The two stood looking at one another for a few more moments before Jake shook his head in wonder. 'I prayed and prayed for this, Sky. From the day I first met you I knew I wanted to marry you some day. But I thought there was no way someone as beautiful as you could want someone like me.'

Sky chuckled. 'Why, because there's no way I'd want someone good looking, mature, Godly and,' she bit her lip, 'who loves me with a much deeper love than I could have imagined?'

He appeared surprised. 'You think I'm good looking?'

'I do.'

He looked doubtful, but like a magnet she came to him and

reached a hand to his face. 'I love your dimples; laugh lines, or whatever you call them. I love your eyes, the way they can tell me what's going on in your heart. I love your ears. They're so neat and perfect. I love everything about your appearance. But most of all I love you; who you are; your heart. You make me feel so secure and so unsettled all at the same time. I feel like I want to run from you and hug you all at once. No one's ever confused me or filled me with as much joy as you do.'

Jake stared at her, speechless, then pulled her into his arms. No words were necessary. She could see the fullness of his heart in his eyes.

Finally he pulled back. 'Okay, I'm feeling confident now. Let's go and watch this documentary that could make every guy in the world stalk you.'

She threw her head back and laughed. 'I won't notice any one of them, Jake. I promise.'

'Not even me?'

'Only you.'

***

Everyone was still praying about coming to the camp centre as a family. The more they talked about it, the more the idea grew on them.

Starre wished she knew what to do. Her leave finished the following day and she needed to return home. Bruce said he couldn't keep her position open indefinitely. The airing of the documentary had brought in a lot of extra funding, but also a lot of extra animals. Bruce said donations had poured in, but a lot of people had been hoping to see Regal Zion too.

She watched as Prince and Sky stood with the horse Prince had bought for her. Little Cloud was a beautiful creature. Sky would obviously love to live there too; to be closer to her horse and to Jake. She would also be with both her adopted father and

208

her biological father.

It just makes so much sense, God, she told him. *I'd love you to provide the money.*

She watched as Prince helped Sky onto her horse. Unsurprisingly, Sky had a natural way with horses, the way she was a natural at everything she put her hand to. The family had watched her diving in the pool yesterday, perfecting backflips and somersaults that had them gasping.

And as Starre had watched, her heart had swelled with love for the girl. How could she have been jealous of her? Refusing to forgive stole life, but forgiveness set the heart free.

Running feet sounded from near the hall. She turned and her mouth dropped open. Chase was coming toward her, running steadily, like he had as a child, as though nothing could stop him. He still the wore the brace, but there was no sign of his limp.

When he reached her he lifted her and swung her around in his arms. 'Starre, will you marry me?'

Her eyes widened, her heart pounding. 'Yes, of course. But—'

'No buts.' He let out a laugh. 'We've just had the best news. The documentary was a hit. We have so many requests for the story—publishers, television programmes, cinema companies. And the money they're offering is phenomenal. We could build ten camp centres like this one!'

Starre felt as though her heart was going to beat right out of her chest. She couldn't speak.

'It's true.' Chase grinned as a loud shout of joy and triumph came from somewhere near the horses.

Starre managed to find her voice. 'I guess we're all about to be called in for another meeting.'

He held her back. 'Not yet. I want you to myself for a minute first.'

She grinned. 'What for?'

He put his hands either side of her face and kissed her

passionately. Then he looked deep into her eyes. 'I want to marry you, to have children with you—'

'But I thought you couldn't have children.'

Red crept up his neck and into his face. 'It was a possibility, but at my last appointment it was confirmed I can.'

Starre laughed with joy. 'Chase, why didn't you tell me?'

He shrugged. 'I wasn't going to come out with it in any normal conversation. Especially not before we were engaged.'

'And we're engaged now.'

He nodded. 'Not for long. I want to get married soon! And I think we should call our first child "Grace".'

She raised her eyebrows. 'Really? Even if it's a boy?'

Chase didn't miss a beat. 'Yes. Even if it's a boy.'

She frowned. 'But—'

His face split into a grin before he let out a hoot of laughter. 'I can give as good as I get, Starre Clements. And don't you forget it!'

She couldn't help laughing with him as they headed into the hall, ready to discuss the future of the Clements family and the newly formed camp centre, 'Hope of Zion'.

***

Sky gazed around at her family as they ate the evening meal and her heart was full. Charles and Marion had joined them for the celebration. Jake sat beside her, holding her hand.

Blaze was at the head of the table where the family had insisted he be placed. He was the one who had been a parent to them at the loss of their mother and the one who had first given his life to God. His heartfelt prayer of thanksgiving at the beginning of the meal had touched them all.

Beside him sat Bonnie, her startling blue eyes as beautiful as ever. The older she grew, the more expressive they became and the more her burn scars blended into her ageing skin.

Next sat Prince and Rachel. Prince was saying something to

her, as she looked over at Paul. Paul looked lost in his own world. *Probably dreaming about Kathina*, Sky thought with a smile.

Alexa, Seton and Blythe were play-fighting across from him. They had a piece of screwed up aluminium foil from the top of one of the salad bowls. Seton was pulling on Alexa's shirt as she tried to get away, foil in her hand. Then she tossed it to Blythe, who giggled as she missed it and Seton made a dive at it.

Philippa was out with the horses. She'd barely left Regal Zion's side since the day he'd arrived at the camp centre.

Then came Roy and Misty. She held their youngest in her arms and was dimpling at something Roy was saying softly into her ear. Benjamin was out with Philippa; no doubt still following her around, telling her all about Victorian Dream, his mother's amazing circus horse.

Starre sat quietly beside Chase, taking in everything in her quiet, thoughtful way.

Storm and Tori were listening, captivated, to Beauty and Chappy tell stories about their daughter, Olivia.

'So I'm settling her into bed one night,' Beauty said, while Chappy put on an innocent expression and acted out what she was saying, 'when she says, 'Mummy, before you go can you just tell me something?' So I sit down on the bed and say, 'Yes, what would you like me to tell you?' And she looks up at me with innocent eyes and says, 'Everything you know.''

Sky couldn't tell whether Storm and Tori were laughing more at Beauty's anecdote or at Chappy's perfect mimicry of his little girl.

Chappy grinned mischievously and looked sideways at Beauty. 'So either Olivia thinks her mother isn't very intelligent, or she is a very clever little cherub who knows how to manipulate her mother into letting her stay up late.'

Beauty turned to him and he immediately moved back and spoke quickly. 'Of course I believe it's that she's very clever. Just like her mother.'

His wide-eyed, dramatic expression had the group laughing again and Beauty joined in, shaking her head at him. Sky knew he had the ability to keep campers entertained for hours.

She watched the way Tori then looked down at her own little girl, cradled close to her chest. Storm smiled down at her and their eyes met for a moment. For a girl whose mother didn't know how to model love, it seemed to come naturally to Tori.

Sky turned to Jake. 'Are you sure you know what you're getting yourself in for?'

He grinned and nodded. 'Yes. I've put up with you for years, haven't I? Surely your family can't be any harder to cope with.'

She poked him and he laughed before capturing her hand in his and pulling her close. 'I've never wanted to be a part of a family so much before.'

Sky snuggled against his chest, gazing around at everyone. She marvelled at the way God had brought them all to this point. He'd always had a plan for the Clements family and he'd brought it to fulfilment. He'd worked in each individual and met their needs in a way only he could. He'd wooed them and brought them to himself. He'd forgiven them and taught them to forgive. And now, under this evening sky, he'd brought them all together again. All individual, all his children, and all part of the amazing plan of forgiveness.

ALSO BY JENNY GLAZEBROOK

Blaze in the Storm
Bonnie's world is happy and carefree until Blaze Clements and his horse-crazy family arrive from the circus. Is believing in God the only way to make sense of the tragedy that strikes?

Heart of Thunder
Beauty Clements hates her name – along with everything and everyone. What will it take to get through to her? Can God's love and forgiveness free her from her past?

Clouds of Prayer
Prince Clements captured Rachel's heart the moment he left the circus and rode into her school. But she is a minister's daughter and Prince has no time for God.

Mist of the Morning
Roy can't work out if clumsy Misty Clements is clever and manipulative or if she is just as lost in the world as she seems. What is she hiding from him?

Clinging to Rainbows
Tori is running from her past and from the law. Disguising herself as Storm Clements seems to be the only answer to her survival. But what if Storm finds out?

Author's Note to the Reader

Thank you for walking the journey of the Clements family with me. I enjoyed writing this series, creating characters God brought to himself despite their pasts, hurts, failings and self-focus.

I believe God wants you and me to know him and his forgiveness. I have personally experienced this and pray you also experience the freedom that comes from God's forgiveness and the release of burdens we and others place on ourselves.

As we see throughout the Bible, and is expressed clearly in Luke 19:10, Jesus came to seek and save the lost. He came that we may live life to the full. (John 10:10)

I pray that you may be found in him and that your eyes will be open to his love and grace. May you be restored in your relationship with God and may you shine his love and light into the lives of others.

May you allow God to write the story of your life, and may you know that it truly does make a difference in the lives of your friends, family and all those you come in contact with.

I know that until we reach heaven we don't usually get to see the big picture; all the details of our lives that come together to make a beautiful, complete story. But I have confidence that God is working all things together for good in your life when you live for him. (Romans 8:28)

Thank you for your support. I'd love to hear from you. You can contact me through my website.

www.jennyglazebrook.com

www.ingramcontent.com/pod-product-compliance
Lightning Source LLC
Chambersburg PA
CBHW031243120726
47905CB00002B/704